TOO YOUNG TO
DIE

ROBERT O. SABER

WILDSIDE PRESS

Complete and Unabridged

CONTENTS

PART I

The Flesh Peddlers

One

Bank Holiday

SHE WAS A PRETTY thing, apparently of about high-school age, with short, curly blonde hair and a figure which managed to look sexy in spite of her casual plaid blouse, blue skirt and brown-and-white saddle shoes. She passed in front of the plate-glass window behind which I was sitting, waited on the corner for the traffic lights to change, then slowly crossed the street and strolled toward the Cosmopolitan Bank.

In front of the bank's panel of doors are three wide stone steps. She climbed them slowly, pausing a moment on each step as though she had all the time in the world and, when she reached the top step, she turned and faced the street. She made a pretty picture, standing there in front of the glass doors, and I figured her as a young kid waiting for a boy friend.

I stretched lazily, carried my empty cup to the counter, and gave the hash-slinger a dime for a refill. When I got back to my table, the blonde kid was still on the top step but, I noticed, she wasn't looking up and down the street in the semi-bored, semi-nervous way that most young girls do when waiting for a date to appear.

9

Instead, she had her purse open and was peering intently into a small mirror.

Clark Street was pretty dead. A few delivery trucks were pounding back and forth. A sprinkling of decrepit characters were wandering around in the morning sunshine, trying to soak up some of the ultra-violet and oxygen their flophouses didn't supply. A few cops were on the street, most of them beating leather for the district station a half-block away and looking as though their feet were already sagging under the burden of the eight-hour shift coming up. As usual, much of the traffic on the corner revolved around the bank, for it was Friday, the day most of the smaller merchants deposit their week's receipts and make withdrawals to meet salaries. For a while, a constant stream of people entered and left the bank, then the stream thinned and became a mere trickle. But the girl kept her place in front of the doors and continued to peer into the mirror, at the same time fiddling with the ends of her hair.

I finished my coffee slowly and lit a cigarette.

My office was on the floor above and I knew that I ought to be opening my mail and thinking of ways to make a buck, but the girl was beginning to bother me. That's one of the crosses a private dick has to carry. After a few years of prying into other people's business, analyzing their motives and trying to outguess them, a guy gets so he starts adding and subtracting people automatically. Without thinking, I'd started doing it to the girl—and she didn't add worth a damn.

For one thing, her hair was perfection and didn't need all the attention she was giving it. For another, she was standing right smack in the center of the bank's entrance, where she was in the path of everyone going in or coming out. If she were merely wasting time or waiting for someone, she should have had sense enough to stand to one side. She looked like a sweet young kid, but sure as hell wasn't acting like one.

I observed her narrowly for several minutes, then it hit me: The business with the mirror was merely a cute act. She wasn't studying her hair. *She was watching someone inside the bank!* For a long moment, the fact wallowed sluggishly in my mind, making no sense at all. I had seen her cross the street and approach the steps. She hadn't been following anyone. But perhaps that had been an act, too.

I sat up straight and took a good look at the other people on the sidewalk below her. About twenty-five feet to the left of the entrance, a slim fellow in a natty brown suit was standing on the curb, his back to the street, apparently reading a newspaper. While I was studying him, he lifted his eyes casually, glanced at the girl, then darted a second glance toward the corner. I followed the glance and spotted another fellow, shorter and heavier but equally well-dressed, who was loitering unobtrusively beside a parking meter. His back was toward me, so I couldn't see his face, but it was obvious that he, too, was trying to give the impression of reading a newspaper.

Frowning, I pushed back my chair and stood up. At the same instant, the girl lowered the mirror, slipped it into her purse, and snapped the purse shut. She stepped casually aside, descended one step, and smiled across the street, almost directly at me. As though her movement had generated an electric impulse, Brown Suit and Short Guy folded their newspapers in unison and looked at the bank entrance. I looked, too.

One of the glass doors swung outward and a tall, cadaverous man in a black suit and black felt hat appeared. He had a thin, pock-marked face, a bumpy beak of a nose and heavy-browed, somber eyes. He stood on the top step a moment, as though pausing to fill his lungs with the clear morning air, and then descended slowly, moving with the deliberate, grave air of a man who carries a large portion of the weight of the world on his shoulders. Immediately, the door behind him swung outward again, expelling a slight, dapper old gent in a beautifully tailored gray suit. He had an aristocratic, Kentucky colonel-ish sort of air, and, if I hadn't known better, I'd have figured him as a wealthy elder statesman who'd paused briefly in the bank maybe to clip a few coupons.

I muttered, "Red Dog Pyle! What in the hell—"

In his day, Pyle had had an international reputation as a big-time con man. He had gotten his start back in the early days of transatlantic crossings by establishing himself as a wealthy vacationer who liked to play cards and, on the last night out, fleecing the wealthy suckers aboard by getting them involved in an innocuous-seeming card game called Red Dog. He had gone from card-sharping to the big con, specializing in imaginative real estate deals, stock swindles, jewel switches and just plain fortune-hunting. Rumor had it that he'd made a million bucks during his gay career, and had tossed it away betting on slow horses and fast women. The last I'd heard, he was too old and too well-known to be active in the rackets, and had retired to a small town in Ohio where a daughter was supporting him. But he sure as hell wasn't anywhere in Ohio now. He was in Chicago, right in front of my eyes—and making an exit from the Cosmopolitan Bank . . .

While I stared at him, he posed delicately on the top step, dipped into the breast pocket of his suit for a silk handkerchief, touched it briefly to his forehead, then folded the handkerchief with a quick gesture and stuffed it casually into the inside pocket of the jacket.

"I'll be damned," I murmured. "He's fingering that guy with the black hat!"

THE FLESH PEDDLERS

The whole play was over in a matter of seconds, and it was done so smoothly that, if I hadn't spotted the act and guessed what was happening, it would have escaped my notice completely. While Pyle was doing the handkerchief business, the cadaverous, black-clothed man descended the steps and crossed the sidewalk toward a black Cadillac sedan parked at the curb.

Brown Suit and Short Guy started toward him, walking at a casual pace like idlers who had suddenly made up their minds to move on. They timed it nicely. He was in the middle of the sidewalk when they converged upon him. Short Guy, because the prey had headed his way, acted as the wire and, apparently by accident, bumped against Black Hat, caught him as he stumbled off balance, and began an anxious apology. At the same instant, Brown Suit passed beside them, carrying his folded newspaper in one hand. They did the trick too fast and too skillfully for me to follow it, but I knew that Short Guy had dipped into the victim's inside pocket and had slipped the loot to Brown Suit, who was rapidly striding away with it concealed in the folds of the newspaper.

Brown Suit reached the corner at the same time that a Radio Cab halted for a red light. The cab caught his eye and, with barely perceptible hesitation, he stepped into the street. The cab had "712" lettered on its door and carried Illinois plates 441-243. While Brown Suit was climbing in, I got out a pencil and an envelope and jotted down the numbers.

In the meanwhile, the girl had come down the steps and was approaching Black Hat from the rear. She reached him at about the same time that Short Guy was concluding his apologies. She touched the man's arm to attract attention, and I saw her red lips bend into an anxious smile then move quickly as she asked him something. He smiled benignly

13

and bent gravely toward her as though he were a little hard of hearing, and her lips repeated their quick movement. Short Guy, released from his victim's attention, made a clean break simply by walking rapidly away. Black Hat pursed his lips as though pondering a matter of grave importance, then murmured something and pointed a long finger in the direction of the Loop. The girl nodded her head and smiled brightly, obviously expressing her thanks, then skipped lightly toward the corner.

It all happened with the speed and precision of a well-oiled machine. By the time I had got through the cafeteria's revolving door and reached the street, the man in black had climbed into his sedan. As it moved slowly from the curb, I ran into the street, trying to get a look at its rear plate. I made out Illinois 669-122. I jotted it down hurriedly on the envelope and looked around for Pyle.

He was not in front of the bank. I looked north and south on Clark Street. No Pyle. I ran to the corner and looked east and west on Chicago Avenue. Pyle had disappeared—and so had the girl.

I cursed softly. The caper was obvious now. The girl, Pyle, Brown Suit and Short Guy had been working together as a jug troupe. Pyle had been inside the bank, had seen Black Hat make a sizable withdrawal, and had fingered him for the two wires. The handkerchief business had been a signal, a means of telling Short Guy and Brown Suit the location of the victim's wallet. The girl, of course, had been keeping track of Pyle's movements with the mirror and, by watching her, the two wires had known when to get ready for the play. Also, she'd functioned as a stall, after the lift had been made, making it possible for Short Guy to make a smooth break before it occurred to Black Hat to check his pocket. Altogether, it had been a hell of a slick operation!

I grinned suddenly. Hell's bells, I'd been looking for a

way to make a buck, and here was a made-to-order set-up.
For once in my career, I wouldn't have to start at the tàil end
of things and scratch my way backward, for I'd been on the
case before the victim knew he'd been hit and I had seen the
whole swindle unravel.

All I needed was a go-ahead from the victim—and, of
course, the usual retainer—and I was in a position to wrap
the case up in a hurry. I still had to tag the participants and
make a stab at recovering the loot but, with the start I had,
the job ought to be as easy as shooting fish in a barrel. Good
jug troupes are rare these days; one operating locally would
surely start tongues wagging. Pyle's being in the deal would
make it easier for me, too, for an old-time con of his stature
couldn't circulate in a city like Chicago without arousing a
whisper or two. The smart guys had a way of keeping an ear
to the ground. All I had to do was buy a few drinks for the
right boys and I ought to be able to pick up enough information to sing the whole song, draw a complete picture, and
maybe even quote chapter and verse.

It took me a split second to make up my mind. I'd play it
smart. I'd give Pyle to the cops and take some quick info in
exchange. I headed for the Chicago Avenue police station.

I found Sergeant Haney Peters in the detectives' room,
typing a report with one finger. He glanced at me, frowned
slightly, and went on typing. I pulled an empty chair over
and sat down. When he got to the end of the page, he released a sigh of disgust, rolled the page out of the battered
machine, added his initials with a pencil, and tossed the
sheet into a tray behind him. He sat back and stared at me.

"What's on your mind, Carl?" he asked, lifting a bored
eyebrow.

I shrugged. To my mind, cops are like people. Some of

them carry a torch, some of them carry a cross, and some of them are out strictly for dough. I'd had dealings with Peters in the past, and I knew that he was as square as cops come —but who the hell can support a family on $395.00 a month?

"I got a deal cooking," I said carefully.

"Yeah?" He straightened in his chair and pulled in his belly so he could cross his knees. His fat face was a little more florid than usual, but his eyes narrowed perceptibly. I knew that he was interested.

"Maybe you can help," I suggested.

He snorted. "Maybe, hell. Sure I can help. Why the hell else would you be here?"

"You can save me some chasing around. I've got a couple license numbers. I'd like a run-down on them."

"Yeah?" He lifted an eyebrow. "What's the story?" Meaning, of course, what was there in it for him.

"The information isn't worth more than a fin. As a matter of fact, the whole thing is speculation. I may get a case out of it—and I may not."

"What kind of a case? Some guy cheating on his old lady, as usual?"

I wrinkled my nose at him. "Hell, sarge, don't you think private dicks do anything besides chase deadbeats and wayward wives? Only last week I tipped you to a guy who was wanted for larceny. This may be the same kind of deal."

"Larceny, my eye." Peters blew through his lips. "The case got thrown out."

"Well, that wasn't my fault," I pointed out. "How about it, sarge? It's worth a fin to me—and I'll toss in a piece of valuable information."

"What kind of information?"

"The kind that'll convince the captain that you're on the ball." I got out the envelope. "I want to know who owns a

16

black Caddy sedan carrying plates 669-122, and I want to know where I can locate the driver of Radio Cab number 712, which carries plates 441-243. I want to contact the driver immediately, if not sooner."

Peters pursed his lips and frowned. "You want a lot for a fin."

"It's a simple trace."

"The Caddy license may be, but the other isn't." He considered. "Tell you what. If you've got a ten-spot, I'll stick my neck out and tell the cab company to order the driver to burn-gas down here to the station." He eyed me innocently. "That way, he'll get here in a hurry and you won't have to hang around on a corner, waiting to spot him."

I sighed. "Okay, sarge."

"Give me them numbers again."

I repeated them and he jotted them down on a memo pad. Swinging ponderously around to the phone on his desk, he dialed a number. He talked briefly to central headquarters in a bored tone, made notes on the pad, then dialed another number. His voice became gruff and official. I grinned and shook a cigarette out of my pack. Like a dancing master barking orders to a *corps de ballet,* he began informing an official of the Radio Cab Company that the driver of cab 712 was wanted by the police and had better get to the Chicago Avenue station in a hurry. When he hung up, I laughed and got out my wallet.

"You didn't have to read them the riot act," I said. I handed a tenner to him. "If they radio half of that to him, he'll think it's a gag."

"He'll get here in a hurry," Peters promised. He pushed the bill into a shirt pocket, then frowned at his notes. "The Caddy is registered in the name of Doctor Richard Williams, 71 Delaware Place." He eyed me suspiciously. "What's the angle, Carl? This Williams is nobody to monkey with."

17

"Never mind the advice," I told him. "You've got my dough. Give me the information."

Peters moved his thick shoulders in a so-be-it gesture. "The driver of cab 712 is named Paulo Moreno. The company's radio room says he's on a trip out north some place. As soon as they contact him, they'll have him scoot down here."

"Good enough, sarge. Thanks." I stood up.

"Hey, how about that tip?"

"That's right." I lit my cigarette and exhaled slowly, trying to decide how much to tell him. "Red Dog Pyle is in the neighborhood."

"The hell you say!" Peters stiffened. "Where'd you see him?"

"Coming out of the bank a few minutes ago."

"The bank!" His voice jumped an octave and he came out of his chair as though he'd been shot. "The *Cosmo?*"

"Yeah." I smiled into his flushed face.

"By God, Carl, if you're bulling me—!"

"Cross my heart, sarge. He's wearing a light gray suit, a black string tie, a pearl-gray felt hat, and—"

He didn't wait for me to finish. "Jesus H. Christ," he blurted in an angry, wounded tone. "You sit here yakking about some goddam license numbers to me, and Pyle's probably a mile away! If he pulled a job in this neighborhood—!"

I grinned and ducked out of the station.

Two

Follow That Blonde

FROM THE CURB IN front of the police station, I looked across the street to the second floor of the Chicago-Clark Building, where large gold-leaf letters on a narrow window proclaimed:

CARL GOOD
Private
Investigations

During a period of temporary optimism, a year before, I had the sign put on the window of my two-by-four office on the theory that troubled people, exiting from a tussle with the police, would spot it and pound a trail to my office door. The lettering had taken a fifty-buck bite out of my bank account, and it had been money down the drain. To my knowledge, the sign hadn't brought me a cent's worth of business but, with sun glinting off it, it sure as hell looked pretty.

A Radio Cab came bowling east on Chicago Avenue and cut suddenly into a parking place in front of Maurie's saloon. Without bothering to turn off the ignition, the driver

climbed over the front seat, yanked open the door, and sprang onto the sidewalk. He was a small, thin-haired guy in a green sport shirt and wrinkled cotton slacks. He trotted past me, looking very worried, and I noticed his lips were trembling a little. I put out a hand and caught him by the arm.

"Paulo Moreno?" I asked gruffly.

"Yeah." He stopped dead in his tracks, as though the touch of my hand had congealed him.

I led him back to the cab. "Let's see your trip sheet," I said.

"Look, officer, what's this all about?" he quavered nervously. "I ain't done nothing. Honest to God, officer, I only been on the street a couple hours this morning, and I ain't even—"

"Your trip sheet," I interrupted. "You keep one, don't you?"

"Sure, sure, I got one! If you'll tell me what the gripe is—" He opened the cab and got out a square of fiberboard to which a ruled sheet was clipped. With trembling hands, he handed it to me. There were only two entries. The first showed that he'd picked up a fare at the Palmer House and had taken it to 61 East Goethe. A second fare had been picked up at 1100 Lake Shore Drive and dropped at 846 North Wabash.

"About a half-hour ago," I said in a hard voice, "you picked up a fare at the corner of Chicago Avenue and Clark Street. He wore a brown suit and was carrying a newspaper."

"Sure, sure, you're right," he admitted. "I didn't have time to write it down! I hardly finished the trip when I get a call from the company that the cops—"

"Where'd you drop him?" I broke in.

"At Diversey and Pinegrove. Honest to God, officer, I

20

woulda written it down, but the company said I was in trouble and that I hadda—"

"How much trouble you're in depends on how you cooperate," I told him. "What the hell is at Diversey and Pinegrove?"

He looked blank. "What do you mean?"

"Don't play dumb. You took the guy to a definite address, didn't you? You didn't just drop him on the street corner."

"Sure, I did! When he got in, he told me to take him to Diversey and Pinegrove. When we got there, I asked him whereabout on Diversey he wanted to go, and he said the corner was good enough. I swear to God, officer, them's the very words he—"

"Look." I forced myself to speak slowly. "You let the guy out on the corner. Where'd he go?"

"Into the Ottawa Arms. You know, that hotel—"

"Come on." I pushed him into the cab. "Let's see how fast you can get me there!"

He scrambled behind the wheel while I climbed into the back. The cab jerked away from the curb and headed east at a wild clip. At Dearborn Street he went through a red light, made a sharp turn, and nearly crashed into a garbage truck.

"Watch the lights!" I snapped. "You want to go home in a basket?"

As he eased up on the gas, I noticed that his flag was up. I leaned over and slapped it down. He jerked his head around as though I'd hit him between the ears. "Hey, you mean you're gonna *pay* for this?"

"City expense," I retorted. "Mind your driving!"

"Yessir, officer, but I sure wish you'd tell me what the hell this is all about! The guy didn't kill nobody, did he, officer?"

21

"We don't know," I said shortly. "Did you talk to him during the trip?"

"Some." He jerked his head into a series of nods.

"What about?"

"Well, when we started he was doing something with his newspaper, so I kept my mouth shut, but by the time we hit the park I noticed he was just sitting there looking out the window. So I said it was a real nice day for this time of year, and I told him that some people were saying that the reason our weather seemed to be changing was because of the atom bomb, and—"

"For chrissake," I snorted, "are you hackies still slinging talk about the weather nowadays?"

"Well, that's what we *started* talking about. You wanted me to tell ya, didn't ya?"

"Okay. Skip the weather. What else?"

"He said he hadn't been in the city long and wanted to know what was doing."

"So?"

"So I told him the heat had been on for some time and that most of the spots were crying the blues. He wanted to know what the local guys did for excitement."

"What did you tell him?"

He shrugged. "I told him the city was dead, that the police had everything shut up tight except the bars, and they were only open until two in the a.m."

"You're a goddam liar," I said flatly. "What kind of excitement was he looking for?"

The cab was hurtling along the winding drives in Lincoln Park, and the driver made a point of keeping his eyes straight ahead. "How would I know?" he asked, shrugging again.

"How would you like a couple of days in the can?" I asked.

22

"Jesus, officer, what do you want from me? I was just doing a job, wasn't I? How'd I know that—"

"What kind of excitement was he looking for?" I repeated.

"Oh, hell." It was an admission of defeat. "Girls, if you want to know."

"What'd you tell him?"

"What do you think I told him? I tried to give him a good steer. I told him that the joints were full of chippies, but all they'd do is take his dough and give him a pat on the cheek in return. Hell, you know how it is, officer. The cheap hustlers have been run out of town, and all that's left is a lot of cold-blooded dames who're out for the buck. They take everything and give nothing. I did him a favor. I gave it to him straight."

"Crap."

"It's the God's truth—"

"You know goddam well you gave him a couple numbers to call."

"Numbers? Where would I get numbers? You think I ain't got enough troubles without going out and asking for more?"

The cab shot out of the park and ground to a stop on Diversey near the Ottawa Arms Hotel. I got a five-dollar bill out of my wallet and dropped it onto the seat beside him. "Listen, Paulo—" I leaned my arms on the back of his seat. "I'm not city police. This is big-time stuff you're mixed up in. You want to play this smart. If you're tagged as an accomplice—or for aiding and abetting—you may wind up in a federal pen. You don't want that to happen, now do you?"

"Christ no." His voice grated like glass on sandpaper. "You mean you're F.B.I.?"

I didn't nod, but I didn't deny it either. I held his eyes

23

with mine for a long moment. "What did the guy want, Paulo?" I asked softly. "Tell me the truth."

He squinted a little, as though trying to see something which was far away. Whatever vision his mind conjured, it wasn't good. He shivered a little, then said reluctantly: "He wanted a kick."

"Horse?"

He shook his head. "Morphine, he said."

"What'd you tell him?"

He bit his lip and shrank into the corner of the seat.

"What'd you tell him?" I demanded ominously.

"I gave him a number, one I got from another cabbie." It came out of him in a squeaky whisper, one syllable at a time, as though it were being torn from a deep internal organ.

"What was the number?"

"Delaware 7-2124."

"Who gave it to you?"

"A guy I know. He's okay. Honest to God, he's—"

"What's his name?"

"Sammy Villa."

"He work for the same outfit you do?"

"Yeah."

I nodded. "The guy you brought out here . . . You're sure he went into the Ottawa Arms? Did you actually see him go in?"

"Sure, I seen him. I was parked right here when he got out and started across the street, and just then I got a flash to call in. I was setting here, listening to the boss screaming something about how I was in a jam with the cops and had to tear down to the police station, and I saw him cut across the corner and head for the Ottawa Arms' canopy. Take a look, yourself. I'd have had to be blind to miss him, wouldn't I?"

He was right. The hotel's green canvas canopy extended clear across the sidewalk and from where the cab was parked there was an unobstructed view of it. Even with his mind on other things, he'd have seen Brown Suit entering the hotel.

"Okay, Paulo," I said. "Keep your trap shut about this. Understand?" I got out of the cab.

"Hey, your change!" He waved the fiver. "The fare's only a buck-fifteen—"

"Buy yourself some smokes."

I crossed the street and stood under the green canopy, mentally debating ways and means of proceeding. I knew how the guy had been dressed, but I didn't know his name. I didn't know what, if any, room he was occupying. I was reasonably certain that the troupe would rendezvous in a hurry to inspect and divide their loot, and the spot selected for the rendezvous could have been the Ottawa Arms. But Brown Suit had asked the cabbie where he could get a kick. That tagged him as a stranger in town, an addict whose supply was running low, one who needed a quick lift, one who was worried about a new source of supply. It was entirely possible that, feeling a need for a shot after the strain of the job at the bank, he'd decided to stop at his room for a bite of the needle, then had gone on to a rendezvous somewhere else.

In any event, time was running out on me. I had to get to them in a hurry, before the loot was cut up like a tray of canapes, but I was in the awkward position of a guy whose doorbell is ringing while he's got his pants down. I had to jump—and jump quick—but in which direction?

I had about decided to wander into the hotel and try my charms on the desk clerk, when a Yellow Cab screeched to

25

a stop at the curb behind me. I glimpsed a blonde girl in the back seat leaning forward to hand money to the driver. My heart did a do-se-do and, without looking around, I walked slowly toward the hotel's brass-edged doors. Her heels beat a quick click-click on the sidewalk behind me. As I pulled the door open and stepped aside, she brushed past me with a small smile and a murmured, "Thanks!" I got a swift sniff of a pleasant cologne and a good look at her face. It was the right girl, the one I'd spotted in front of the bank. Coincidence? Luck?

She hurried ahead of me, but I quickened my step and reached her side as the door of the elevator slid open. She stepped in quickly—and I followed. It was a small, oak-paneled cubicle, the kind which operates slowly, safely, automatically, and without three shifts of salaried attendants. I smiled at her and punched 9, which was the top button on the control panel.

"What floor did you want?" I asked politely.

She smiled nicely at me.

"Five, please."

I punched 5. The door whished shut, a motor hummed, the cubicle rose. When it reached the fifth floor, it stopped and the door slid back. She stepped out hurriedly and turned left. The dor whished shut. I jammed my thumb against a red button labeled *STOP* and held it there for thirty seconds. Then I punched *DOOR OPEN*. Obediently, the door slid back.

I inched my nose around it. The corridor to the left was deserted. I stepped out, letting the elevator door close behind me, and prowled silently down the aisle, pausing for a moment before each door. They were dark, thick, solid panels, well-fitted and without the usual ventilator-grill. I heard nothing, nothing at all.

Feeling frustrated, I continued to the end of the corridor

26

where a small, reddish *EXIT* sign glowed, and pushed back
the door. It led to a narrow flight of concrete fire stairs. I
stepped past it cautiously, listened for several seconds and,
still hearing nothing, I eased the door almost shut, keeping
it open a crack with the toe of my shoe. Peering through
the crack, I got out a cigarette.

Before I could touch a match to it, a plank of light fell
across the corridor and the blonde darted out of a doorway.
She flung a wild-eyed glance in my direction, but it was a
split-second, agitated glance and she didn't spot the narrow
crack through which I was watching her. Like a startled
gazelle, she turned and ran down the corridor, kicking her
heels out in the odd way that girdled girls do when they are
making haste and think themselves unobserved. She went
past the elevator, ran to the far end of the corridor, turned
a corner and vanished from my sight. I flung the match
away and raced after her, reaching the corner just as a door
clicked firmly shut. There were eight doors. She could have
entered any of them.

Cursing softly, I ran back to the room she had left so hurriedly. The door was open a half-inch and a thin slat of yellow light lay across the corridor's carpeting. I listened for
several seconds, then pressed gently against the panel. It
moved a grudging two inches, giving me a glimpse of a green
wall, a framed lithograph of an urban scene, and a telephone
stand. In the back of what passes for my mind, a warning
bell clanged dully.

I pressed against the panel again, a little harder than before, and a section of a fairly large living-room came into
view. I could see half of a boxy, Lawson-type sofa, a window
draped with floral-printed chintz, a lot of beige broadloom,
and a good two-thirds of a glass-topped coffee table. The
coffee table was littered with ash trays, loose cigarettes,
match packets, a nut dish, a pair of soiled white gloves, a

27

girl's brown leather purse, and what appeared to be a paper canister.

I stared at the purse a moment, then drummed my knuckles lightly against the door. I waited another moment, then, ignoring the frantic alarm signal beating in my brain, I stepped into the apartment and closed the door. I could see the whole living-room now, as well as the open door of a closet, the doorway of a bedroom, and the arched entrance to a small dinette and kitchen. Except for the coffee table, everything was neat and orderly. As if a maid had cleaned the place not too long before.

Frowning a little, I walked to the coffee table and eyed the purse. It was open, and without even touching it I could see that it contained a capacity load of the miscellaneous knick-knacks and cosmetics which girls like to have handy for social emergencies. The edge of a thin red wallet was visible. I fished it out with one finger, flipped it open. It contained thirty-four dollars in bills and a charge-plate notched for use at several of the big department stores. Reading the metallic letters in reverse, I learned that it belonged to Miss Betty Brandt, Ottawa Arms Hotel, Chicago. I returned the charge-plate to the wallet, and pushed the red wallet back into the purse.

The paper canister caught my eye. It was the size of a scouring powder can, had a polished metal top in which a large slit had been die-cut, and bore a large white label on which, printed in crimson block letters, was the legend: *DONATE TO THE BROTHERHOOD FOR SERVICE.* Near the bottom, also in crimson, was an afterthought in smaller type: *Thank You!* I picked up the can and shook it. It was very light, but it rustled faintly. I grinned. If the Brandt girl had been soliciting contributions for the brotherhood, she hadn't bothered with nickles and dimes; to me, the rustling sounded like folding money. I set the canister down and stared at the purse again. A thought was nibbling at my mind.

Usually a girl and her purse are inseparable. Its contents are highly personal. Most girls hug them under their arms, hold them in their laps, clutch them by a strap, keep them handy to their hands, even carry them to the bathroom with them. It was possible that Betty Brandt had come in, changed her clothes, and decided that a switch of purses would make her outfit more harmonious—but obviously this wasn't a purse which had been discarded. The wallet was an evidence of that; also, people simply don't leave charge-plates lying around, not if they have any sense at all. The purse, then, strongly suggested that its owner was still in the immediate vicinity. Involuntarily, I stiffened and looked around. *Perhaps she was still in the apartment.*

The thought sent a chilling tremor up my spine, and, suddenly acutely apprehensive, I strode toward a door which was ajar—and pushed it back. It revealed a pink-tiled bathroom. Without entering, I searched it with my eyes. The plastic shower curtain was still damp near its bottom and, even as I stared at it, a drop of water formed slowly and, with a faint kissing-sound, dripped into the empty tub. I could smell soap.

A heavy towel, still damp and rumpled, lay on the floor in front of the washbasin. On the basin itself, there was an open box of powder, a lipstick, an ornate bottle of twisted crystal, and a piece of tissue which bore a brilliant red smudge. Mentally, I added it up: Merely minutes ago a woman had showered, dried herself, stood on the towel in front of the mirror while she applied cologne to her body and make-up to her face . . .

A vivid picture of the blonde, wild-eyed and agitated as she ran into the corridor, flashed across my mind. I sucked in my breath and my heart began to do a nervous buck-and-wing. I knew, suddenly, what I was going to find in the bedroom.

I was right. It was a large room, luxuriously furnished and full of feminine frills and pastel colors. The only note of disorderliness was the slim figure which, clad in black panties and a filmy black lace bra, lay sprawled across the satin covering of the bed. The long pale legs were twisted slightly, as though she had tried to lever herself up, and her thin arms were stretched toward eternity with pathetic desperation.

I leaned over and laid the palm of a hand against the flat V between her small breasts. The skin was soft, smooth and faintly warm. I kept my hand there for what seemed like several minutes, but I could feel no heartbeat, could sense no flutter of respiration. Yet there was no blood, no visible wound, no weapon in sight. Sliding my hands under the body, I lifted it slightly and bent down until my eyes were level with the bed. The white sheets beneath her were unstained.

I released her gently, went to the doorway, snapped on the overhead lights. With the harsh light glaring down upon her, a faint necklace of bruises was visible at the base of the pale column of her neck. I nodded to myself as I fitted the pieces together: She had put on the bra and panties in the bathroom, had entered the bedroom to finish dressing, but had been attacked unexpectedly, strangled, pushed violently onto the bed.

My lips suddenly felt rough and parched. I licked at them nervously and moved around the bed so I could see her face. It was small, oval, featuring a pert nose, wide amber eyes and generous red lips which, even in death, seemed to smile slightly. A thick mass of reddish hair framed her face and lay beneath her head like a coppery pillow. She had been young, I decided, not more than nineteen or twenty—and

30

beautiful, in a sweet, girlish way. The freshly applied make-up made a smooth painted mask of her face, giving it a false maturity, but the glow and freshness of her youth had probably shone through attractively enough in life.

The hair on my neck prickled suddenly as I sensed someone behind me. I started to whirl. Then a rainbow exploded within my head and the floor reached up for me.

Three

Room Service

I WAS IN BED . . .

A woman was beside me . . .

The thought slid into my brain like a long piece of cold, soggy spaghetti and slithered slowly around and over the edges of my stupor. I groaned and moved my legs tentatively. My knees bent reluctantly and I felt the rough surface of a woolen blanket. I also felt the warm satiny-smooth texture of skin.

An exclamation started to bubble toward my lips but, with a caution born of experience, I gulped it back and permitted only a whisper of a sigh to escape. Then I held my breath, wondering if I had disturbed her. I hadn't. The faint rise and fall of her breathing continued without faltering.

I straightened my legs and inched my hips away from contact with her body. The small movement made the bedsprings creak intimately—and my blood froze.

It took my numbed brain a long while to audit the facts and formulate a course of action. The problem seemed to be one of infinite magnitude, and I lay there, completely inert and hardly breathing, while I wrestled mentally with ways and means to escape without waking this woman—without being seen leaving by her. For vaguely, like a bad dream I had had a long time ago, I remembered a reddish-haired girl sprawled across a bed. She had been dead. Strangled. The two words, *dead* and *strangled*, hopped and skipped across my mind, making little sense. The woman beside me was alive. She was not dead. That was clear.

Gingerly, I lifted a hand and felt my head. My arm twinged as I moved it and the back of my head was a thin bubble of pain. I had been in the redhead's apartment. I had been standing beside the bed, looking down at her—when someone had hit me. What had I been doing there? The muck in my head obscured the answer, but gradually a hazy picture of the bank, the blonde and the jug troupe's act floated across my mind. I rubbed my forehead. The woman, the live woman, the one in bed now—how had that happened? For a long while, all memory handed me was a big round 0. Then another question slowly formed: *A frame?*

The question ballooned and brought reality back in a quick, sharp flood. Anger and fear spurted through my body and made me sit up with a bounce and swing my legs over the side of the bed. The abrupt movement made the bed rock like a rowboat caught in a sudden squall and the bedsprings began to creak like an old windmill. Cursing silently, I turned to see if I'd awakened her.

I had. As though she'd been dropped from the third floor of a burning building into a taut canvas net, she flung out her arms and rose a couple feet from the bed with her legs thrashing in a frantic bicycle stroke. Her eyes were wide with terror and her mouth was opening, warning me that a scream was about to shatter the silence.

I flung myself at her as her mouth started to open, but the first note caught me in mid-air. Her nails slashed at my chest and clawed at my eyes. I got a hand over her struggling mouth. The scream died in mid-octave.

33

"For chrissake, shut up," I said hoarsely. "You want the cops climbing in here?"

Her teeth chewed at my hand, her nails tore at my shoulders, and her legs flailed the bed in a dangerous duet as she tried to knee me in a vital spot. Her wild blows, added to the pain in my head, reacted like kerosene on a small fire. My anger flared. For an instant, I forgot her sex and aimed a fist at her belly. I caught the blow before it landed, telling myself that, hell, maybe she was somebody's mother.

"Relax," I rasped. "I'm not going to harm you. Just promise not to scream."

Her mouth worked beneath my hand, trying to get one of my fingers between her teeth so she could chew it off, and her eyes glared at me in a way which was not reassuring.

"Just promise to keep your mouth shut," I pleaded hoarsely, "and I'll release you."

Hate, fear, and desperation glinted in her eyes as, by way of answer, she rammed a knee viciously upward toward my groin. I cursed, caught the blow with the inside of my thigh. Dropping my whole weight onto her, I crushed her beneath my chest and scissored my legs around her thrashing limbs. I had gotten her legs under control and was beginning to relax and try to think when her hands found my hair and tried to remove my scalp by the roots. She was stronger than she looked!

I stifled a howl, struck at her arms, got hold of one of her wrists. I tore the hand away from my hair. The fingers of her other hand tugged harder, sending waves of excruciating pain through my throbbing head. I was forced to release her mouth. I caught her other arm, tore it out of my hair, and forced it cruelly back over her head.

Her mouth gulped a lungful of air and her body tensed as she prepared to hurl a scream into the room. Before it could reach her lips, I rolled my face against hers, found her

34

mouth, clamped my lips over hers. The scream blew into my cheeks, but no one heard it, not even me. Her lips were hard and tight with anger. She jerked her head from side to side, writhed, bit, spat, choked, ground her teeth against mine, and tried every trick in the book until, finally, she was forced to recognize her defeat.

The fight went out of her suddenly.

Her arms and neck went limp and she ceased struggling. Her lips fluttered beneath mine for a moment, then they, too, relaxed. Not knowing what to expect, I continued to hold her for several minutes. We lay there, our bodies glued together with sweat and exhaustion, our mouths joined with fear and distrust. We were both breathing heavily, in very near the same rhythm. Her eyes, a mere inch from my own, seemed more alive than they had in the beginning and less crazed with fear. As I stared into them, they slid shut, then opened again. Her mouth moved slightly under mine, as though, forgetting, she had tried to lick her lips. I felt, rather than heard, a small moan rise within her.

I lightened the pressure of my lips. Her mouth twitched slightly and, again, I felt her tongue travel the width of her lips. I questioned her with my eyes. Her answer was a bleak look of resignation and defeat. Still not trusting her completely, I lifted my mouth cautiously away from hers and stared into her eyes.

"Screaming will get you a lot of loose teeth," I warned harshly.

"Please!"

"I said I'm not going to hurt you."

She rolled her head and stared at me as though seeing me for the first time. I noticed that she had a thin, ascetic face and long black hair which lay in a loose, twisted mass on the pillow. Her eyes, reflecting the afternoon sunlight which angled through the tilted slats of a venetian blind, were large, frightened, hollow, and blackish-brown. Her mouth worked soundlessly for several moments.

"Who . . . who are you?" she whispered at last.

"Dick Tracy," I said bitterly. "Who'd you think?"

"Tracy?" Her forehead puckered in thought.

"I suppose you've got a blank in the head, too," I said sarcastically.

"Yes. I—"

"You make a habit of waking up in bed with strange men? Or didn't your mother tell you?"

"I . . . I don't know what you're talking about . . ."

"No kidding!" I snorted.

"Who are you? What are we doing here?"

"For chrissake," I said. "Don't you know?"

She shook her head. I could feel her tensing expectantly, as though readying herself for a shock. "No. Tell me. What are we doing here?" Her eyes dropped a little and seemed to be counting the hairs on my chest. "I don't know you, do I? We haven't ever met before, have we?"

They were good questions. I stared at her while I arranged the facts in my mind. She was no kid. She was somewhere in her late thirties or early forties, but her skin was clear, her bones good, her face thin but symmetrical. I'd never seen her before. A glance at the room had told me that we weren't in the Brandt girl's apartment, so I didn't know where we were, and—I was convinced—neither did she. Also, she was scared as hell; not as scared as she had been at first, but still thoroughly a-quiver. A private eye, to survive, has to be a fast guy with a hunch, and I had a hunch that she was on the level.

"My name is Carl Good," I said. "I don't think you know me."

As soon as the words were past my lips, I wanted to bite my tongue in half. Leveling with her was one thing; giving

36

her my real name was stupid as hell. How idiotic could I get?

"Oh." She said it blankly. She wriggled her wrists gently, reminding me that I still had them pinioned to the bed over her head. I released them cautiously, watching her the way I'd watch a domesticated leopard. With a weak sigh, she rubbed her wrists, then touched her forehead with the back of one hand in the sort of gesture women use when the fingers are sticky. "Oh," she said again. "Good?"

"Who are you?"

"I'm—" She gulped, colored a little, and made a series of gagging noises in her throat. "I . . . I think I'm going to be . . . sick. Could —?" Her eyes finished the question by groping desperately about the room.

"Sure thing."

I rolled away from her and sat on the edge of the bed. She averted her eyes, as though just remembering the fate of girls who peeked at boys, sat up unsteadily, and got weakly to her feet. Swaying a little, as though walking were a strange exercise to her, she stumbled across the room toward a darkened doorway. She paused a moment, fumbled for the switch, then light flooded her, revealing a pale, mature Diana with small breasts and flat hips. She stood there, leaning weakly against the jamb a moment, then she stepped into the bathroom and the door clicked shut. I soon heard the sound of flushing water.

I cradled my aching head in my hands and mentally cursed my curiosity and chosen profession, my stupidity, my big mouth and congenital bad luck. That done, I got to my feet, crossed the room, and turned on the overhead lights. The room was larger than most bedrooms, but there was a vague emptiness to it, as though it were little used. The carpeting was thick, worn in places, and dusty. The dressers were large, clean-lined and badly in need of polishing. I opened a drawer. It was empty. I opened several more. Except for a Gideon Bible, they were all empty.

I grunted indecisively and began looking for my clothes. I found my trousers, shoes, and socks in a heap on the other side of the bed, looking as though they'd been thrown there in a hurry. I got them and wandered around, looking for my shirt and jacket. I found them on a hanger which dangled from a hook inside the door of an otherwise empty closet.

I punched my arms into my shirt and glared at myself in a dresser mirror as I fumbled buttons into holes. I looked all my 39 years and then some. My face was a crisscross of wavy red lines where clawing nails had carved angry paths, my graying-black hair stabbed at the air like the furious quills of an aging porcupine, and my eyes looked like brown holes poked in a loaf of unbaked bread. With a snort of disgust, I tried to smooth my hair with my hands. I was only partially successful. Next, I rubbed my eyes in a halfhearted attempt to push them back into my head. I looked like hell. No wonder she'd been scared half to death. I felt like screaming, myself.

I walked to the closet and jerked my jacket from the hanger. Beneath it, on a similar hanger, was a small cloud of pale gray fur. I muttered. "Sapphire mink!" My startled eyes flashed the news to my brain and my brain promptly expanded with incredulity. The cash register inside me, equally incredulous, started ringing up dollar signs and large sums which averaged off in the vicinity of seventy-five hundred. Whistling softly, I touched the fur with my fingers. It was as soft as a lover's lie and a thousand times more marketable. I peeked at the label stitched to its lustrous satin lining. *Bonwit Teller.* I whistled and touched the fur again, very respectfully.

That fur was very interesting.

To a private eye, especially to a small-time operator like

yours truly, making the acquaintance of a woman with a sapphire mink coat is better than knowing how to forge a banker's signature to a check. Forgery is a crime and forgers have a habit of getting caught. Women with fancy mink coats, on the other hand, invariably have troubles. They got the coats from doting old jokers who have more dough than sense, and either she or he, sometimes both, usually need the services of a private eye sooner or later—the old joker to make sure his monopoly on the woman's services is really a monopoly, the woman to check on his assets and make sure she isn't marking time when she might well strike out for greener pastures.

It's a hell of a situation when you think about it, but it takes money to make the world go around—and who am I to throw the first stone? A job is a job, the dough I make that way is just as negotiable as the kind I'd make sweating my tail off in a factory. And if you want to know the truth, I'd rather get a line on a situation like that than have an inside tip on which nag is going to win at Arlington. Things were looking like I might be in business.

The idea perked me up considerably and, without hesitation, I strode across the room to where I'd noticed a small heap of feminine clothes. Squatting on the floor beside them, I rummaged through the scented odds and ends. There was a plain, flesh-colored bra and a matching pair of nylon panties, a tricky garter belt of narrow elastic, a black wool skirt, a gaily colored blouse of nylon tricot and, at the bottom of the pile, a black purse shaped like a gift box of cigars, the kind that only holds 25 smokes. With a grunt of satisfaction, I pushed the other stuff aside and unsnapped the purse. Besides the usual female junk, it yielded a flat wallet. Not red. Pigskin.

The wallet was my baby. It contained $158 in assorted bills, most of them as clean and crisp as though they'd been

39

minted especially for her and, in plastic windows, a series of identification cards. According to the cards, Mrs. Royal C. Greene of the Belclark Apartments had extensive credit privileges, was a member in good standing of the Chicago Motor Club, the Illinois Club, the Michigan Shore Country Club and the Columbus Hospital Blood Bank. She was Type O, incidentally.

Her driver's licenses interested me. One, issued in 1950, bore the seal of the State of Wisconsin and had been granted to Patricia Larkin, a resident of Milwaukee, *age*—39, *hair*—auburn, *weight*—110, *height*—5' 3". The other, dated the current year, had been issued in Illinois to Patricia L. Greene, *address*—Belclark Apartments, *age*—43, *hair*—black, *weight*—115, *height*—5' 3". By traveling 90 miles and crossing a state line, Patricia had apparently put on a few pounds, changed the color of her hair and acquired, in addition to a spouse, a lot of charge accounts and, I suspected, quite a few problems.

After tossing the stuff back into the purse and arranging her things as I'd found them, I strolled to the bathroom door and held my ear against the panel. Water was splashing within. I tapped gently. The splashing stopped and she called nervously, "Y-yes?"

"Feeling all right?"

"Y-yes . . . thanks."

"Need anything?"

"N-no." Pause. Then: "My clothes. Would you be good enough—?"

"I'll put them by the door."

"Thanks ever so much."

Allowing for the filtering effect of the panel, her voice sounded clearer and stronger. Grinning, I bent down, gathered her clothes in my arms, and dropped them in front of the bathroom door. I was picking up her shoes and nylons, intending to deposit them beside the clothes, when, some-where else in the apartment, a telephone began to jangle. Sucking in my breath, I let the shoes drop with a thud and sprinted toward the sound.

I left the bedroom in such a hurry, in fact, that I tripped and damned near fell smack on top of the body.

Four

Hidalgo Terrace

HE WAS SPRAWLED ON the other side of the bedroom doorway with his pudgy arms outflung and his beak of a nose pointing straight up at the ceiling. Beneath a square, clean-shaven chin, a wide red mouth yawned—only it wasn't really a mouth. It was the gaping, blood-encrusted wound left by a thin, sharp blade which had whisked across his throat, slicing it from ear to ear.

I fell forward, went down on one knee, caught myself and half-hurdled over the body, narrowly avoiding putting a foot smack into the browning continent of blood which stained the surrounding carpeting.

The phone kept jangling. Locating it on a stand in a hallway, I ran to it and snatched up the receiver. A male voice demanded impatiently: "That you, Tom?"

I stared at the sprawled body and tried to swallow the dry lump in my throat.

"Tom?" the voice crackled. "Hello, Tom?"

"Yeah," I said gruffly.

"How're things?"

"Okay."

"You got the stuff?"

"Yeah."

"Say, what the hell's the matter? You sound kind of—"

"Getting a cold," I interrupted. "Call me back in an hour. I'm busy right now."

"Look, Tom. Just tell—"

"In an hour," I repeated firmly. Then I depressed the dojigger on the phone with a fingernail, got out my handkerchief and wiped the receiver thoroughly before dropping it back onto its cradle.

Turning on all the lights I could find, I studied the dead guy. He had been a short, stocky man with a thick shock of gray hair, a swarthy, full face. Judging by the quantity of gold in his teeth, he had been a regular patron of a good dentist. He wore an expensively tailored suit of beige gabardine which sported handstitching around the lapels and a crust of dried blood around the edge of the collar. He had been somewhere in his early fifties, maybe a little older, but not much.

I got as close to him as I could without stepping onto any of the bloody carpeting and reached for his right arm. I lifted it gently. It moved easily, much more so than I'd expected. Perhaps the fact that the room was hot explained the lack of rigor. When I released the arm, it plopped back onto the carpet and bounced a little, as though made of a good grade of rubber. Something glittered. I pulled the arm toward me, twisted it, stared at the hairy fingers on his hand. There was a wide gold band around his little pinkie which was set with a nice piece of ice, a very nice little piece of ice. Around four carats, I guessed. I let the hand bounce against the carpet again.

The weapon wasn't visible. Mostly to satisfy my own curiosity, I felt carefully around the edges of the body without finding anything. Apparently the murderer had kept it as a souvenir.

TOO YOUNG TO DIE

The man's suit jacket was unbuttoned. Being careful to disarrange things as little as possible, I slipped a hand inside and teased out the contents of the breast pocket. There was a soiled envelope addressed to Mr. Royal C. Greene, a leather cigar case initialed R.C.G., and a flat packet wrapped in brown paper, sealed at each end with reddish wax. The packet bore no name, no address. I put the envelope and cigar case back where I'd found them, and transferred the packet to my hip pocket. I was considering an inspection of his trouser pockets when the sound of the bathroom door opening reminded me of my companion. I arose, circled the body, and strolled into the bedroom.

Her back was to me and she was standing in front of a mirror, arms raised, adjusting the mink jacket about her shoulders. Clothes, a comb and make-up had done wonders for her. She had swept the black hair back from her face in a severe patrician line and twisted the ends into a bun. Her thin face looked blasé, perfectly controlled, less bloodless. She even appeared taller, slimmer, and faintly aristocratic. Hearing my step, she whirled to face me. A glance told me that she'd got back her poise, too, and had made up her mind to give me a quick, fast brush.

"I thought you'd gone," she commented coldly, barely flicking her eyes at me.

I tipped my head toward the bathroom. "I was waiting for you to get through."

She shrugged, implying that the natural functions of others bore no interest for her, and made an imperceptible adjustment in the hang of the jacket. With a cool glance at me, she pivoted neatly on the toe of one shoe, essayed a step toward the door, and spoke what she thought was her exit line: "Well, I'd better be going. Thanks for . . . for everything, Mr. Good."

"Where are you going?" I asked casually.

44

She took a second step. "That's none of your business."

"I'm afraid it is."

"I think not." She said it firmly. With a slight twitch of her hips, she took a third step and headed for the door.

"We'd better talk this over," I suggested.

"There's nothing to discuss, nothing at all." By the arch of her neck, I knew that she'd shaken her head positively and tightened her lips into a hard, negative line. She reached the doorway. I watched her grimly. She turned to fling what she intended to be her final remark: "Goodbye, Mr. Goo—" My name ended in a short gasp, followed by a frantic clatter of her heels and a stifled shriek.

I leaped across the room, hurdled the body, pulled her onto her knees, and slapped a hand over her mouth. "Cut out the dramatics," I snapped. "I warned you to stay put. It's your husband, isn't it?"

"Y-yes!" Filtered through my hand, the word was barely intelligible.

I took my hand away. "He's dead."

Her eyes rolled like loose marbles. "Oh, my God! Poor Roy! What have I done—!"

"Did you kill him?" I demanded bluntly.

"Me?" The tip of her tongue stabbed at her lips, trying to moisten them. "Are you crazy?"

"Sometimes I wonder."

"But . . . but . . . oh, my God!" She shuddered. "This can't be happening to me. I must be dreaming. It's like a horrible nightmare. First that . . . that in . . . there—" Her head made an agonized dip toward the bedroom. "—and now . . . this. My husband . . . dead. What are you trying to do to me—?" Her voice rose dangerously.

"Look, Mrs. Greene—" I pulled her away from the body and pushed her toward a couch. "I know you're shocked. So am I. But you've got to get a grip on yourself. This is murder. Understand? Your husband isn't merely dead. He has been murdered."

"I didn't kill him!" She jerked away from me, avoiding the couch.

"Did he come here with you?"

"Of course not. He was—"

"Did he know you were coming here?"

"No. He couldn't have. *I* didn't even know I was coming here!" Her eyes searched the room wildly. "I don't even know where I am. Whose apartment is this?"

"I wish I knew," I told her. I walked to the window and peered between the slats of the venetian blind. I could see the green curve of Lincoln Park, the golden statue of Alexander Hamilton, and the concrete front of the Meat Packer's Institute. We were in a building south of Diversey Parkway, but we weren't in the Ottawa Arms. This building was taller than nine stories.

"You killed him, Mr. Good!" she accused. "You drugged me and brought me here and . . . and you knew he was dead. No one was here except us. You're the one who brought me here. You're the one who—" The words tumbled off her thin lips like startled coins from a jackpot. Even a one-eyed idiot could have seen the way her mind was working, could have sensed the way she was trying to manipulate the deck and deal herself a handful of aces. "—you came out here while I was in the bathroom and . . . and you talked to him. I could hear you. But I didn't know it was Roy. I didn't realize it was my husband. When you started arguing—" Her dark eyes were narrow and bright and her chin was rising with wild, frantic hope.

"Crap," I told her. "Pure crap—and you know it."

"Prove it."

"Not me." I shook my head. "That's a job for the cops."

"Then call them. What are you waiting for? You should

46

have called them immediately, instead . . . instead of—" She stopped and bit her lip.

"Instead of what?"

"Instead of putting on such an act. You didn't have to . . . to humiliate me so!"

"So I've put on an act," I said disgustedly, "and you've been humiliated. How about your husband? How do you think he feels?"

"He's dead—and you murdered him!"

"You lack the right sound effects, Mrs. Greene." I sat down. "Listen to me. I'm a private investigator. I was working on a case and stumbled over a dead body. A girl's body, not your husband's. Someone—the murderer, probably—attacked me and knocked me unconscious. The next thing I knew, I was in there"—I indicated the bedroom—"with you. That's the truth. I can't prove it, but it's true, and—"

"You're lying—!"

"Shut up and listen. We have a problem, a mutual problem, and I'm trying to state it fairly and clearly. I don't know how you got here. I don't know anything except that you were in that bed with me and that this body has been lying here for several hours. It hasn't been officially identified, but you say it's your husband's. Okay. I'm willing to believe it. But my business brings me into regular contact with the police. I know how they operate, how they think, and what their routine involves. I also come into contact with a lot of guys in the rackets. I know how they operate, how they think, and what damned cute ideas they get. That's why I want a little sense out of you. I don't think you realize what a hell of a spot you're in."

"W-what do you m-mean?"

"This. Forget about me and try to visualize the set-up. Your husband is lying here dead. Someone killed him. That someone also arranged for us to be together in there." I

47

pointed at the bedroom. "To get me here, they had to go to a hell of a lot of trouble. You haven't told me where you were before . . . well, before you woke up in there, but I suspect that they brought you here, too, and it wasn't easy. It was damned dangerous for them, and the only reason they did it was because they thought it'd be some kind of insurance for them."

"B-but—"

"No, not insurance," I corrected myself. I frowned. "They weren't worried about the murder rap, apparently. If they were, they'd have tipped the police and the place would be blue with cops. They had some other reason. A reason which they considered important. It was a reason which necessitated having us wake up in the same bed." I snapped my fingers. "A picture! They took a picture. For chrissake, that must be it."

"*What?*"

"They photographed us. In bed together." I eyed her sardonically. "That means *you're* the one they're after. I just happened to be handy. What are you mixed up in?"

"Nothing. You must be crazy. You're trying to twist things—"

"Twist, hell. They're already twisted. Can't you see that?"

"No." She faced me, one hand on a hip and her legs spread. "You killed my husband, Mr. Good. When they ask me, I'll tell the police all about everything. They'll believe me."

"All?" I asked. "You'll admit publicly that you came here like a two-bit floosie and climbed into bed with a total stranger? How else can you explain my being here? You'll have to prove that you knew me, that we were having an affair, that your husband found out about it. One lie will lead to another, and you'll be going around and around the liar's circle."

48

"They'll believe me. I'll make them believe me."

"You'll tell the cops that you heard me fighting with your husband, that you were in the same room with the body— and that you didn't run for a phone and call them?" I taunted. "You will like hell. If you want your story to hold water, call them right now. They won't like your running out and letting the *corpus delecti* get cold."

"I will call them," she cried. "As soon as I get out of here. I'm afraid of you. I daren't call them from here. You threatened me. I was afraid for my life." She struggled for phrases and managed to sound like a third-rate actress on a no-fee TV show. She knew her ship was leaking in a hundred places, but there was too much brass, too much pride in her to let go. "I . . . I'll tell them that you tried to keep me here. You wanted me to be your accomplice. But I escaped. I called them from the first telephone I could find. I'll tell them you fought with him over me. They'll give you the third degree. They'll force you to confess."

"Sure," I said sarcastically, "and after they listen to you they'll get sick from laughing. You've been listening to too many half-crocked radio shows. The homicide boys aren't stupid. They're not run-of-the-mill cops who break into a sweat when they have to spell out the words for a parking ticket. The cops who'll check your story will be smart boys. When they get through, you'll look ridiculous as hell, and so guilty that even your best friend won't know you. Try to plaster me and all you'll get is a fat headache."

"I'm through talking," she snapped. "You killed my husband. I'm going for the police." She flung past me and headed for the door, digging her heels into the carpet as though trying to leave a permanent impression.

"Hey—wait!"

"*Goodbye.*" The door slammed.

"Goddammit to hell," I commented bitterly.

49

TOO YOUNG TO DIE

I sat there a moment, glaring at Greene's dead body. Then I got busy. I was reasonably certain that she had no intention of calling the cops, but there was a possibility that someone else might come nosing around, and I had a great desire not to spend the next couple of days on an oral merry-go-round answering a lot of questions to which I had no answers.

Let me make this point clear: In spite of what it says in the newspapers, the less a guy has to do with the cops the better off he is—and that goes 100 per cent, in my experience, whether he's innocent or guilty. I don't say it pays a guy deliberately to destroy evidence. But when a guy is a small-time private eye, and a major crime like murder is involved, and he isn't related to a high-powered lawyer who'll defend him for nix, and in addition he knows it's dimes to doughnuts that somebody's banging together a frame that'll fit his neck as well as anybody else's—hell, I wouldn't hesitate a second. And, as a matter of fact, I didn't.

I dashed into the bedroom, stripped the bed of its sheets and blanket, and folded them together with extreme care so as not to fan any loose hairs or pieces of skin onto the floor. When they were folded, I skinned the cases off the pillows, added them to the pile, and carried them into the kitchen. Spotting a vacuum cleaner in a corner, I wheeled it into the bedroom, hooked it up, and gave the area around the bed and dresser a thorough going-over. Back in the kitchen again, I detached the dust bag from the machine and carefully shook its contents into a large paper bag.

The bathroom came next. I bent and stretched and strained until everything in sight had been polished with a dry towel, and that included all the mirrors, porcelain, chrome, the inside of the medicine cabinet, and even the enameled seat of the john. When I finished, I was dripping sweat from every pore and my shirt stuck to my back as though it had been cut from adhesive plaster. I felt reason-

50

ably sure, though, that any fingerprints she might have left had been obliterated. As a final touch, I cleaned out the drains of the washbasin and bathtub, removing several long black hairs, and wrapped the cake of soap she had used in a damp towel.

I gave the bathroom and bedroom a final critical inspection, then got a shopping bag from the kitchen junk closet and stuffed it with the sheets, blanket, pillowcases, towels and the sack of vacuumings.

With the bag under my arm, I walked carefully around Greene's body, checked the living-room to make certain that I'd overlooked nothing, then started for the door. The telephone caught my eye. I stopped, studying it nervously. I'd handled the receiver. Had I removed my prints? I thought I had, but I couldn't remember doing it. I took out my handkerchief, picked up the receiver, and gave its smooth black surface a quick once-over. As I replaced it on its cradle, the dial attracted my attention. Within a black circle at the center of the dial, the phone's number was printed in white letters: DIversey 9-2247. The phones in most apartment hotels bear an extension number. This one had none. It was a private line, one which was in service, yet the apartment showed no signs of occupancy. Odd.

I opened the door cautiously and stepped into a wide, carpeted corridor. The door bore brass numerals: 1603. I closed it firmly, located the fire stairs, and trotted down them to the twelfth floor. Then I rang for the elevator and rode down to the lobby.

The lobby was spacious, modern and deserted. I crossed it swiftly, hugging the bag close to my side, and stepped into the street. The green canopy of the Ottawa Arms was twenty feet to my left. I blinked at it, then looked around, searching for the name of the building I'd just left. I found it on a polished brass plate beside the door: *Hidalgo Terrace Apartments.*

I was looking for a cab when heavy feet pounded the sidewalk behind me and a big hand caught my arm and spun me around.

"There you are, you bastard!" Sergeant Peters roared triumphantly. "I knew damned well you'd still be around." He licked his thick lips as though getting ready to seduce a sixteen-year-old immigrant. "I've got news for you, Good. You're under arrest!"

Five

Dust To Dust

"ARE YOU NUTS?" I snapped. I jerked my arm loose. "Under arrest for what?"

"Questioning." Sergeant Peters uttered the word with great satisfaction and reclamped his hand on my bicep.

"Questioning about what?" I demanded.

"Murder." Peters grinned hugely. "Thought you'd run out on me, eh?"

"Oh, for chrissake." I said it disgustedly, like a man being deeply wronged by a grave miscarriage of justice. While my mind, doing quick mental gymnastics, realized this was a very sticky moment: I not only had the shopping bag in my hand but the packet I'd snagged from Greene's body was in my pocket. Examination of either could be damned embarrassing, especially if Peters started playing the part of a police sharpie.

"Tough titty, huh, Carl?" His tone was frankly gloating.

"Tough, hell," I snorted. "I'm a legitimate private operator. You haven't a goddam thing on me."

"You can sing that song to the captain." He grinned again, squeezed my arm in a bone-crushing grip, and urged me toward the corner where a squad car was parked.

"Look, sarge, for chrissake, you're making a mistake," I protested. "You've known me for years. I'm on a case. My time is valuable. Can't this be squared?" It was a weak motion to fix but, as I've mentioned before, Peters was usually vulnerable to a quick buck and I figured it wouldn't hurt to try.

"Nix." Peters shook his head reluctantly and forced me into a trot. "Captain ordered you brought in."

"For what?"

"Questioning."

"You could at least tell me who's been killed."

"A babe in the Ottawa Arms."

"I don't know any babes there."

"You usta, maybe. The dead-wagon's got her to the morgue by now."

"Look, sarge, is this on the level?" I sounded very sincere. "Did somebody really get killed in there?"

"Damned right." He flung open the rear door of the squad car. The driver, a young cop I didn't know, turned and eyed me interestedly. "Get in," Peters ordered. "Don't try any tricks."

"Who was the babe?" I asked. I held onto the open door and stared toward Diversey Parkway, where a steady stream of cars was funneling toward Lincoln Park. I wondered what would happen if I heaved the shopping bag over the squad car and into the middle of the passing traffic. Two or three cars might run over it and mash it. But there was a chance that they'd swerve around it or that the thing wouldn't burst. Even if it did get smashed, the sheets and towels would certainly be retrieved and I'd have pinpointed police attention on them. There'd be Greene's packet, too. With considerable reluctance, I discarded the idea.

"Ask the captain," Peters said brusquely. He jabbed me in the kidneys and ended the problem of the shopping bag by snatching it out of my hand. "Get in, dammit. You think we got all day?"

I got in.

The ride to the Chicago Avenue police station was too brief for much constructive thinking, but it gave me time to push things into a sort of mental order. I know that trying to force things is a sucker's pitch; if the dice are falling wrong, they're falling wrong, period, and the game either has to be played on that basis—or the player had better get out. I couldn't think of a way of getting out, but I did concoct a half-baked story, one just stupid enough to be credible.

The driver ran the squad car into the alley beside the station and parked. Peters, breathing moistly through his mouth, opened the door on his side and climbed out, taking the shopping bag with him. I got out slowly and slammed the door, making a minor production of the act. Then I stood still, fished for a cigarette, fumbled in a pocket for matches. I glanced toward the windows of the Chicago-Clark building. I thought I spotted movement in Morrie Tannen's office, but I wasn't sure.

"Come on, come on," Peters urged, grabbing my arm.

"Can't I even light a smoke?"

"Do it inside."

With Peters clutching my arm, I walked into the station. He dragged me toward the door of the captain's office and drummed his knuckles on the polished wood. A gruff voice, sounding somewhat vinegary, ordered: "Come in!" Peters licked his lips, then turned the knob.

Captain Burt Stone was pacing the floor behind his desk, looking very unlike a cop. His gray suit was two hundred bucks worth of hand-stitching and the pale blue butterfly tie which bobbed beneath his brick-red face looked like at least twelve-and-a-half bucks of somebody's money. He frowned slightly and tightened his lips as we crossed the

55

room, eyeing me as though the way I'd been kicking the gong around lately was hurting his ears.

"Sit down, Good," he ordered. "You, too, Peters."

Peters pushed a couple of chairs nearer the captain's desk and the three of us sat down.

"What's this all about, captain?" I asked. "I've always been cooperative. Why send a squad after me?"

"Sorry if you've been inconvenienced." He said the phrase pleasantly enough, but I sensed he didn't mean it. He continued to eye me as though I were Bad Boy and he were Peck. "Where'd you find him, sergeant?"

"I caught him ducking out of the Hidalgo Terrace apartment building—" Peters began.

"Ducking, my foot!" I interrupted indignantly. "I came out the front door and this poor excuse of a—"

"Shut up, Good." Stone's voice was mild, but there was a definite edge on the words. "I'll listen to you later. Continue, sergeant."

"Well, sir, like I said, he came out of the apartment building, carrying this shopping bag and looking like he was in a big hurry, and—"

"What's in the bag?" Stone asked. He looked hard at the bulging paper sack and jerked an eyebrow upward.

"I don't know, sir," Peters admitted. "I figured—"

"It's none of his damned business, nor yours either, captain," I said flatly. "The contents of that bag are highly personal and pertain to a case I'm working on. You can—"

"I told you to shut up," Stone snapped. "Either keep your mouth buttoned, or I'll have you confined to a cell until I'm ready to listen to you. Is that clear?" His blue eyes bored into me.

"Sure, but—"

"No buts. Just shut up." He returned his gaze to Peters. "Go ahead, sergeant."

56

"Well, I figured I'd better get him here in a hurry, like you ordered, captain, and leave the bag to the guys in the lab, just in case it contains anything important."

"Did you have any conversation with Good?"

Peters shifted nervously and glanced at me. "Some, sir."

"What about?"

"He wanted to know what the charge was. I told him you wanted him for questioning."

"What else?"

"Well, he gave me a hard time, sort of, so I mentioned that a girl had been found dead in the Ottawa Arms. He said he didn't know no girls there. Then I put him in the car and brought him straight here."

"Did he try to buy his way out?"

"No . . . not exactly." Sergeant Peters lowered his head a little and squinted down like a man who is deeply interested in the condition of his shoes.

"What the hell do you mean by that?"

"Well, sir, he said he was working on a case, and that he hated to take time to ride to the station, and wanted to know if it couldn't be fixed. I said no, of course." A virtuous note entered Peters' voice, sounding somewhat lost and unfamiliar there.

I grunted skeptically but made no verbal comment.

Captain Stone darted a glance at me, then, smiling slightly, said: "See what's in the bag, sergeant."

Peters obeyed with alacrity. He pulled out the sheets, unfolded them carefully, holding them suspended from his arms. Captain Stone sniffed. Peters gritted his teeth and pulled out the pillowcases. He shook their wrinkles out, examined them minutely as though searching for an elusive bedbug, then shrugged and tossed them onto a chair. The blanket came next, then the towels. He frowned worriedly and his color pinkened.

"Looks like nothing but a lot of dirty laundry," he muttered.

"Check for laundry marks, you fool," Stone suggested.

"Yessir." Peters re-examined the sheets and pillowcases. "They're rubber-stamped 'Hidalgo Terrace', captain. He musta swiped them outa the building I saw him coming out of."

"What else is there?"

"A bag of something." Peters bent, got the bag of vacuumings, and held it in his hands. "Want me to open it?"

"Of course, dammit." Captain Stone sounded impatient. "Better use my desk." He cleared a space.

Peters opened the bag, peeked into it, and, looking a little dubious, up-ended it over the captain's desk. Clumps of fuzzy dirt plopped onto the polished wood, sending up a cloud of dust. Peters made a throaty noise and shook the empty bag like a tired woman waving goodbye. Captain Stone sucked in his breath, wrinkled his nose like a man become conscious of a horrible stench, and sneezed violently. The blast blew part of the dirt off his desk and agitated the rest into a swirling mist of dust. "You goddam fool—!" Captain Stone roared. He sneezed again. The remaining dirt swished around and settled toward the floor. "Get that goddam dirt out of here!" Captain Stone bellowed.

I suppressed a grin.

"You told me to put—" Sergeant Peters began.

"Get it out!" Captain Stone ordered furiously. "Open a window! Get some air in here, you fool!" He sneezed again, then glared at me. "Why didn't you say something?" he demanded. He brushed pettishly at the sleeve of the gray suit. "You knew that crap was in there!"

"You told me to button my lips," I pointed out.

"Get a broom, sergeant," Stone ordered. "Sweep that dirt up!"

"And put it back in the bag," I added. "It's my property, you know."

"Your property!" Stone echoed. Impossible as it seemed, his face got redder. "What the hell good is that goddam dirt?"

"It's evidence," I retorted. "It may not be good evidence any more, now that you've managed to get most of it spread around your office, but I laid out dough for it and I intend to keep it. Tell Peters to put it back in the bag."

The captain's jaws worked like a cow with a tough cud to chew. Peters, looking sweaty around the forehead, ran out and came back with a broom and a dustpan. "Put it back in the bag," Stone ordered in a strangled tone. "And when you get it in the bag, you can stuff the goddam bag down Good's goddam throat!"

I grinned. "Better call a couple more cops, captain," I said. "I don't think Peters can handle that assignment very well."

Stone scowled at Peters, and Peters glared at me. With a gesture which smacked of fury, Peters slapped the dustpan at the paper bag and succeeded in sluffing half of the dirt back into it. Grumbling, he made another pile, scooped it up, shook it into the bag. During this procedure, Stone scowled at the back of Peters' head and drummed his knuckles on his desk.

When Peters finished, I said very carefully: "I'm a licensed private investigator, captain, and I'm working on a case. To me, time is money. I'd appreciate knowing what you want with me."

Stone's anger vanished suddenly. He sat back and almost smiled. "You mean you don't know?" he asked silkily.

"I can't even imagine what this is about," I told him. "Peters said a girl had been killed. What does that have to do with me?"

Captain Stone's smile broadened. "Why, we think you killed her," he said.

"Nuts."

"Why not? It figures."

"This ought to be good," I said sarcastically. "How does it figure?"

"Glad to tell you, Good, glad to tell you." He peeled cellophane from a fat cigar and moistened the tobacco lovingly with his lips. "For a private dick who's supposed to be smart, you left a trail a mile wide. But facts are facts. To begin with, you came in here with a cock-and-bull story about Red Dog Pyle being in the neighborhood, and you talked Sergeant Peters into tracing a couple license numbers for you. That would have been all right, but you made Peters phone a come-in for the taxi driver and you picked him up outside and made him take you to the Ottawa Arms." Stone had a tricky way of jiggling one eyebrow. He jiggled the left one now. "Right?"

"I'm listening," I retorted.

"First you impersonated a police officer and questioned the driver about one of his passengers. That's a misdemeanor. Then you impersonated a federal officer. That's a felony." Stone chuckled softly. "You aren't the first private dick who placed his license in jeopardy by pretending to be a cop but, by God, you're the only one I ever heard of who was so goddam dumb that he tossed a cab driver a five-spot and told him to keep the change! That cabbie spotted you as a phony and flew back here like a bat out of hell and told me the whole story."

"I didn't tell him I was a cop and I didn't say that I was a fed," I snapped. "The conclusions were his own."

"The cabbie described the guy you were chasing and swears that he left you in front of the Ottawa Arms," Stone went on. "Another witness spotted you in front of the joint

60

and saw you follow the girl into the building. The desk clerk saw you get into the elevator with her. You went upstairs with that girl, Good—and you killed her!" Stone smote his desk with his fist. "Didn't you?" he demanded, thrusting out his jaw.

"No," I snapped. "The girl I followed into the hotel was a blonde. If the desk clerk was watching, she must have noticed that."

"You followed the blonde upstairs and killed her!"

"Like hell! The girl that got it wasn't—" I stopped abruptly, realizing the trap I'd stepped into, but it was too late.

"So she wasn't a blonde!" Stone roared. "What kind of hair *did* she have, then?"

"Green hair, pink eyes, and lavender skin, you son of a bitch!" I stood up and leaned my hands on his desk. "I don't have to take this kind of crap, Stone. Book me if you're going to, but do it damned fast—otherwise I'm walking out of here."

Stone cursed fluently, describing me as a person who, if half his choice phrases were true, could have found ready employment in a sideshow of freaks. I let him run from the mouth a while, then I snorted disgustedly, picked up the shopping bag, and strode for the door.

Before I could reach it, he shouted: "Stop, goddam it, before I put a bullet in your back!"

I stopped and turned slowly. He had a gun in his hand and looked mad enough to use it. Peters, standing spread-legged as though his trousers had become suddenly moistened, was pawing frantically at his holster. I grinned tightly and walked back to the desk.

At that moment, a sharp rap sounded on the door and Morrie Tannen opened it and stepped into the office. I felt like running to him and putting a big kiss in the center of his bald head.

61

TOO YOUNG TO DIE

Morrie is quite a guy. He's in his late forties, has a bland, round face, no hair to speak of, wears thick horn-rimmed glasses, and walks with a slight limp, the result of a childhood injury to his left leg. He has the reputation of being a shrewd, unscrupulous, shyster lawyer, dealing mostly with the lower elements of society, but I like him. He's smart and can be trusted. His office is next to mine, and I knew that he practiced criminal law through choice, not necessity; he'd tried corporation law and had been bored stiff by it. As for dealing with crooks and outcasts—what the hell, they have a right to be heard in court, and who else would a criminal lawyer deal with, anyhow?

Shyster or not, Morrie was my idea of a good, practical mouthpiece. That was reason number one why I felt like kissing him. Reason number two was this: by virtue of his contacts with the so-called underworld, Morrie knew as much as anybody about the location of the fleshpots, gin-mills and gaming joints, the personnel of the ruling syndicate, and the working methods of the machinery which controls the cops, the prostitutes, the books, the dealers, the short con and the big con, the morphine and gauge peddlers, and all the other lucrative rackets. It was all as familiar as breakfast cereal to Morrie—more familiar, maybe—and I sure as hell needed that kind of information.

"What's going on, Carl?" Morrie asked mildly. He peered at us through his thick glasses. "You in trouble?"

"Get the hell out of here!" Stone shouted. "Throw him out, sergeant!"

"Morrie's my lawyer. I have a right to be represented by counsel," I interrupted. I grinned at Morrie. "Am I glad to see you!"

"I was looking out the window and saw the squad car bring you in," Morrie explained. In a brisk counsel-at-the-bar tone, he asked: "What is my client charged with, captain?"

Captain Stone looked apoplectic. "He's just being questioned!" he shouted. "I haven't charged him with a damned thing—yet!"

"He's trying to tag me with a murder," I told Morrie. "He hasn't told me who has been killed, but I think it was a babe at the Ottawa Arms hotel. He sounds like he wants his picture in the papers."

"Goddam it, I've got a right to question anybody I please!" Stone roared.

"That's right," Morrie agreed. "But you will question him according to the law, not in a back room and at the point of a gun. He has a legal right to have counsel present, and he can refuse to answer if you get out of line." Morrie peered at me. "How about it, Carl, are you willing to be questioned?"

"Why not?" I asked.

"Fine." Morrie nodded and drew up a chair. "Let's proceed in an orderly fashion, captain."

Captain Stone flung his gun into a drawer and sat down heavily. For a moment, he glared impotently at us, then, with a shrug, he bit into his cigar and jerked a thumb at Peters. "Send in a stenographer, sergeant," he ordered. "I'm taking a statement from Good."

Morrie looked at me questioningly. I shrugged. A patrolman appeared with a stenotype machine. Sounding like a man with an inner fury, Captain Stone dictated the opening data, identifying the parties, then he stared at me and said: "I'm asking for a complete statement of your activities this morning, Good. Any objections?"

"No."

"Start talking, then."

I began with the scene I'd witnessed in front of the Cosmopolitan Bank and described the tricky play of the jug troupe. Then I detailed my visit to the police station, quietly emphasizing the fact that I'd paid ten bucks for services rendered. I knew this would alienate Sergeant Peters as far as my getting any future information from him was concerned, but I was sore and didn't care. Stone made bubbling noises when I mentioned the payoff, but he didn't interrupt. I repeated my conversation with the taxi driver, including, for the record, some of my suspicions and conclusions. Stone grunted once and Morrie looked thoughtful. I described my wait in front of the Ottawa Arms and the arrival of the blonde.

"I rode up to the fifth floor with her," I said, "but I out-smarted myself by not getting off with her. By the time I got the elevator door open again, she'd disappeared. So I walked down the corridor to the fire stairs and waited. She came out of 514 almost immediately and ran down the corridor. I ran after her, but I couldn't figure out which room she'd entered. I walked back to 514. The door was part-way open and I could see a purse and things on a table. I figured something was out of pitch, but it was none of my business. I decided to clean up another case I'm working on and to try to spot the blonde later."

Stone muttered something one-syllabled.

"One of my clients is hankering for a divorce," I went on rapidly, "and I've tailed his wife to the Hidalgo Terrace building a couple of times. I figured I'd better check there, as long as I was in the neighborhood, and it was a good thing I did. The maid told me there'd been a lovers' rendez-vous there this morning. For twenty bucks, I bought the sheets, towels, and pillowcases which were in the bedroom, intending to take them to a lab and have them examined for traces of hair, body oils, lipstick stains, smears and the like. I planned to confront my client's wife with the lab report and to put the fear of God into her by threatening to display her dirty linen in court. But your heavy-handed handling of the evidence, which was in that bag, has put me on the spot. You've bitched up the whole deal for me."

Stone snorted. "Which apartment did you get that stuff out of?"

"None of your business."

"I suppose you won't identify the maid, either." There was a sneer in Stone's voice.

"And get her fired?" I returned his stare. "You protect your stoolies, don't you?"

Stone grunted and drummed his knuckles on the desk. "You didn't follow Tina Rogers into the apartment?" he demanded abruptly.

"Who's Tina Rogers?" I asked.

"The blonde. You said you saw her enter apartment 514."

"I said I saw her come out. I let her get away from me at the elevator, but I was standing at the end of the corridor, behind the fire-stairs door, and I saw her come out. She ran down the corridor, disappeared around the bend, and entered another apartment, I think."

"Did you follow her?"

"As far as the bend. As soon as I saw that all the doors were closed, I decided to call it a bad deal and headed for the Hidalgo building."

"But you went back to 514 and snooped around, first," Stone accused.

"I went back, but not to snoop around," I said. "As I told you before, the blonde came out in a hurry and left the door part way open. I glanced in and listened a moment. I heard nothing. For all I knew, she might have run down the hall to borrow a bottle of shampoo, and I didn't want to get tagged as a petty thief. It was none of my business, anyway, so I beat it."

65

"What's your connection with Betty Brandt?" Stone asked abruptly.

"Never heard of her."

Stone snorted disgustedly and lapsed into a brooding silence which lasted for several uncomfortable minutes. "I don't think you're clean, Good," he said finally. "I think you're lying, deliberately and with a purpose. All you private dicks are conniving bastards and, like the rest of them, you're trying to feather your nest at the expense of the police department. I've tried to go along with you guys, but I'm goddam sick of your meddling. I don't like murder. I particularly don't like murder in my district. I think this business you say you spotted at the bank is tied in with a young girl's murder—and, from this moment on, I want you completely out of it. Any idea you had about chiseling a fee, you can forget. Understand? I don't even want to hear you mentioned again."

"I have a legal right to—" I began.

"The hell with your legal rights," Stone said coldly. "I'm captain in this district and if I catch you meddling with this case I'll clap you behind bars so fast your ears will rattle. Now get the hell out of here!"

I looked at Morrie. He shrugged and got up.

I picked up the shopping bag and followed Morrie to the door.

Six

Horse In A Can

"SOMETHING STINKS," I told Morrie when we reached the sidewalk.

Morrie pursed his lips and looked thoughtful. "Why do you say that, Carl?"

"Captain Stone let go too easily," I said. "Maybe he's losing his grip, but I think he's got his tail in the air about something. Didn't you notice?"

"Not especially. He had no right to hold you, you know."

"No, but there were a hell of a lot of questions he could have asked, and he didn't even skim the surface. He sounded to me like a guy with an itch he wanted to scratch, but who was digging around in all the wrong places so people wouldn't know where the bug had bitten him."

"He's probably nervous about things in general," Morrie suggested, shrugging. "A murder in his district won't do him any good, especially if it makes much of a splash in the papers. Since Alderman Merriam started ripping into the tie-up between politics and crime, the police have been trying to keep a lid on things."

"Maybe you're right," I agreed. "Stone was raked over the coals a couple years ago, wasn't he?"

Morrie nodded. "The Citizens' Crime Committee gave him the double-eye."

"What saved him?"

"The grand jury failed to return an indictment." Morrie blinked at me through the thick lenses of his glasses.

"Why?"

"Failure of the committee to prove that Stone's clothes, new brick bungalow and manner of living were inconsistent with his captain's salary." A wry smile tugged at the corners of Morrie's mouth, giving his dour face a childish expression.

"In other words, Stone has strong connections."

"Naturally." Morrie's hand touched my sleeve, almost apologetically. "Don't tangle with him, Carl. There are easier ways of making money."

"He's tangling with me, Morrie." Before he could dispute the accuracy of this statement, I added: "Let's go up to your office."

The only difference between Morrie's office and mine is that his has a small reception room containing an ancient baronial table on which a pile of dilapidated *Life* magazines rests, two stiff-backed chairs for the propping-up of troubled clients, and a scarred desk behind which a thin-lipped frowsy-haired, Whistler's Mother type of secretary operates a typewriter during the day. She gave Morrie an automatic smile as we entered, glanced accusingly at me as though she scented a recent seduction, then picked away at the typewriter animatedly. I followed Morrie into the inner office and dropped the shopping bag beside his desk.

Morrie sat down carefully and peered at the bag. "What's going on, Carl?" he asked.

"Plenty." I made sure the door was closed, then I dripped into the leather client's chair beside his desk. "I think I'm in a hell of a jam."

"Tell me about it."

I gave him the salient details in rapid-fire order. When I described Greene's body, he made a clucking sound with his lips and shook his head worriedly. "If Peters hadn't nabbed me," I concluded, "I'd be pretty well clear, but he spotted me coming out of the Hidalgo Terrace building. As soon as Greene's body is found, Stone is going to remember these damned sheets and towels and he's going to tie me to Greene's killing. Mrs. Greene will be no help. Even though I never saw Greene before, she'll swear we were long-time buddies, or deadly enemies, or even that I killed him because I was hot to get in bed with her. And that's all I'll need. Stone'll have me routed to the chair by Air Express, if not quicker."

"You mentioned a sealed packet."

I took it out of my pocket and slid it across the desk. "This is it. I haven't had a chance to open it."

Morrie weighed the packet in his hand a moment, then slid the point of a paperknife under one of the red seals. When the blob of wax came loose, he folded the paper back delicately and teased the end of the packet open. He peered into it, frowned, then loosened the other blob of wax. He stripped the paper away as gingerly as though he were disassembling an infernal machine, revealing, at last, a rectangular box of black metal. Using the paperknife again, he pried at the edges of the lid. It snapped up suddenly, exposing a fleecy layer of cotton. Morrie grunted and peeled the cotton away, revealing a neat row of flat-topped vials, each protected by a thin buffer of cotton, each filled to capacity with a glistening white powder.

I whistled softly. "Dope," I said. "Heroin, probably."

Without answering, Morrie lifted one of the vials from its nest and unscrewed its cap. He sniffed at its contents apprehensively, then handed it to me. I moistened a fingertip,

dipped it into the vial, and touched a few grains of the clinging powder to my tongue.

"Morphine," I decided. "Highly refined, too."

Morrie took the vial from me, recapped it and returned it
to the box. He replaced the metal lid, then sighed. "I'm
afraid this complicates things, Carl," he said, peering at me
speculatively.

"No," I said, "if anything, it clarifies the situation. Greene
was trafficking in dope and probably cutting in on somebody
else's territory. It explains why he was killed—and why they
framed that bedroom scene of me and Mrs. Greene. Whoever
killed Roy Greene wanted to make sure that his wife kept
her mouth shut."

"But this is very valuable, isn't it?" Morrie flicked his
eyes at the metal can.

"As it stands, it's probably worth ten or fifteen grand," I
admitted.

"It's usual to dilute it for resale, isn't it?"

"Well . . . yes." I shrugged. "Okay, have it your way.
Once this batch is cut and repackaged, it would probably
bring close to $150,000 at the peddler's level."

"If he were killed for trafficking in dope, wouldn't the
killers have recognized the value of this packet and have
taken it with them?" Morrie asked.

"Of course," I conceded, "if the big boys did the killing
themselves. That's a big *if*, though. The chances are that
they hired a couple of guns for the job. You know. They'd
want an airtight alibi in case anything backfired."

"But—"

"Don't forget this, Morrie: these guys were damned busy.
It isn't as though they shot a guy in a doorway. They lured
Greene to that apartment and killed him. Maybe they killed
the Brandt girl, too. In any event, they lugged me from the
Ottawa Arms to the Hidalgo Terrace building, which was

a hell of a lot harder than it sounds. They picked up Mrs. Greene someplace, drugged her, got her to the apartment. Then they stripped the two of us, dumped us in bed, and probably took a few pictures. They had to work damned fast, and every minute they were on the premises increased the chances that they'd be spotted. I think they had a job to do, did it, then beat it without worrying about little details."

"Perhaps you're right." Morrie stared at me owlishly. "You realize, of course, that you should notify the Narcotics Bureau of this immediately."

"Of course," I echoed. I grinned, reached for the box, and rewrapped it in the paper. Then I restored the packet to my pocket.

"As your lawyer, Carl, I must advise—"

"Nuts," I interrupted. "I have to have some kind of a bargaining lever, don't I? Here's what you can do for me, Morrie . . . Check with some of the big boys and find out who Greene was competing with, who his partners were, what kind of a hook-up Greene had to peddle the stuff. I'll call you some time this evening." I stood up and stretched my arms. "I'm going to get rid of these damned sheets."

Morrie nodded. "Good idea."

I took the shopping bag to the basement and set it inside the door of the men's washroom. Then I went upstairs to look for Henry, the gnarled old caretaker who acted variously as watchman, elevator operator and furnace boy. I found him in an empty office on the third floor, reading a religious tract.

"Got a couple of minutes, Henry?" I asked.

He folded the tract and pushed it into his jacket pocket. "Depends," he said. He regarded me sharply.

"Someone left a shopping bag in the basement washroom," I told him. "There are some dirty sheets and towels and

71

things in it. For all you know, they may have been used by someone with a loathsome disease."

"That's right." He nodded wisely. "You want me to get rid of them?"

"Disease is a terrible thing," I said pointedly. "Hospitals usually destroy things like that. It might be a good idea to burn them."

"That's easy, Mr. Good."

I folded a dollar bill and tucked it into his vest pocket. "The sooner they're burned, Henry, the less chance there'll be that anybody touches them."

He winked slyly. "Nobody knows who they belong to, eh?"

"Nobody," I said gravely. "Especially you."

"I just found them, and they looked dirty and smelled kind of bad, so I figured they might be full of germs and things, and I burned them in the furnace so nobody'd get contaminated. Right?"

"Right."

"They'll be gone inside of two minutes, Mr. Good."

"Fine."

He scuttled toward the elevator. I went down one flight of stairs and unlocked my office. There was no mail. I called the phone-answering service. No one had called. Using a wide strip of gummed tape, I sealed the packet of morphine and addressed it to myself in care of General Delivery at the main post office. There were fifteen three-cent stamps in my desk drawer. I plastered them across one end of the packet, then locked my office and left the building by the Clark Street exit. The big letterbox outside Thompson's Cafeteria caught my eye. I dropped the packet into it, then headed south on Clark Street.

The plan simmering on the back burner of my mind was not a particularly brilliant one, but I had to start somewhere and the Player's Club seemed as likely a spot as any. When I entered the joint, a jukebox was blaring a jump version of *Lover Come Back To Me* and a mass of damp-faced men and women at the bar were swaying drunkenly and trying to co-ordinate their wailing voices with the lyrics. I pushed past a couple of Mexican buckos, murmuring pardons, only to find my path blocked by a trio of much-painted, tempo-conscious chicks in skin-tight skirts. I patted the bulkier of the trio on the posterior. She rolled her eyes at me and bounced to star-board without missing a note. The other two caught the movement, did something wobbly with their hips, and permitted me to undulate past.

The air at the rear was thick with the stench of beer and perspiring bodies. The floor was littered. A harried-looking waitress in tight black slacks hurried toward the bar, balancing a tin tray. I waved a buck at her. Without pausing, she snatched the buck and jerked a finger at a small table marked RESERVED. I squeezed past a couple of amorous twosomes and sat down.

The waitress flitted past with a tray of splashing beers and returned a moment later to lean a hand familiarly on my shoulder and demand: "What'll ya have, huh?"

"Scotch with soda and see if Dolly's around, kid."

"Ain't seen her for a couple hours."

"Maybe she's upstairs. Kick the buzzer, will you?"

She scampered away into the crowd, rattling the tray tambourine-fashion to clear a path to the bar. I saw her kick at the signal button which connected with the card room up-stairs, then she screamed at the bartender and banged her tray against the back bar in tempo with the jukebox until he produced the drinks she'd ordered. She dropped a scotch on my table, snatched another buck from my fingers and shrilled into my ear. "Keep an eye on the door!"

The door was an unobtrusive panel in the center of the

73

opposite wall, well within my field of vision. I drained a good slug of the scotch and studied the crowd clustered at the bar. The jukebox had switched to a skittering mambo and there was much bending of knees and elbows. The crowd seemed more dark-skinned than usual and, glancing at the faces individually, it dawned on me that a majority were either Mexican or Puerto Rican. The few Negroes in evidence were female.

The door opened abruptly and Dolly Iola stood posed in the dimly lit opening, one hand on a generous hip and eyes scanning the crowded bar imperiously. She was a large woman, dark-haired and pale-skinned, and built like a Rubens model. In her youth, she had stripped with the best as Dolly O'Day, had married a booze-runner named Ziggy Iola during the heyday of Prohibition and, when he had made the mistake of selling watered liquor to the wrong parties, she'd gathered his estate together and invested it in the Player's Club. The Club had proved a springboard to other lucrative interests and connections. Dolly, in short, was a woman with dough and political know-how; in fact, even though her curves had gone to fat, she was still quite a woman.

I raised my glass and signaled to her. She nodded and came toward me, weaving her hips among the closely packed tables. I noticed that the dress she wore was a smartly cut affair of natural shantung with big gold buttons down the front and a slim golden belt which had a tough time encasing her wide-flung waist.

"Well," she said heartily, easing her hips onto the chair opposite me. "I thought you were dead, Carl."

"Busy," I explained, grinning. "How are things, Dolly?"

"Going straight to hell. Business stinks." She eyed me shrewdly. "What's the trouble? One of your girl friends in trouble?"

"Nothing disastrous like that. How about a drink?"

74

"Save your dough, Carl." She wrinkled her nose. "I got to cut down. I'm getting fat as a pig."

"You're still a lovely hunk of woman. How about a date some time?"

She laughed hugely and her heavy breasts bounced against the edge of the table. "It takes a real man to keep a big girl like me happy."

"Hell, I could try, couldn't I?"

"Sure, sure, any time."

I chuckled. "Maybe I'll surprise you one of these days. Got anything important going on upstairs?"

"A couple of tables of poker. Nothing that can't get along without me for a while. Why?"

"You used to be chummy with Red Dog Pyle, didn't you?"

"Shucks, that was years ago, Carl. I probably wouldn't even recognize the old punk now."

"He looks pretty much the same."

"That so?" A reminiscent gleam brightened her dark eyes and, unconsciously, she prodded at her thick black hair with her fingers. "He used to be quite a dresser. And boy, could that guy spend money!" She shook her head. "The last time I saw him, he had six of us girls up to his hotel and he was tossing money around like it was dandelion seed! No matter what anybody says, he was a good-hearted guy, too. I mentioned once that I needed a coat and he went right out and bought me the best muskrat fur he could find."

"He's in circulation again."

"Who says?" Her eyes suddenly became wary.

I swished another slug of scotch around in my mouth before replying. "I saw him this morning. He's fingering suckers for a jug troupe."

"That's a hell of a come-down."

"The bigger they are, the harder they fall. I thought you might be able to get a line on him for me."

She made Cupie Doll lips and straightened indignantly. "I never stooled in my life, Carl. You ought to know that."

"As far as I'm concerned, he's clean. I want to know who he's working with and where they're holed up."

"Why?"

"I saw them make a score this morning, and unless I straighten things out I'm liable to be in a jam. Captain Stone had me over the coals about an hour ago."

"That louse." She rolled her lips thoughtfully. "You know, I could use a guy like Red Dog. This joint's getting so crumby it stinks, and the game upstairs amounts to peanuts. With a sharper like Red Dog to handle the tables, I could maybe get myself a plushier place over near Michigan Avenue."

"I think Red Dog's looking for a break. He'd probably grab at the chance to go with you."

"Think so?"

"It figures. For a guy like Red Dog, working with a jug troupe is practically desperation. He's too high caliber for that kind of operation. He's older, of course, but give him a good layout and a chance to handle the suckers, and you'd both have a good thing. You'd have to square him with the heat, though."

"I can fix that. Dough squares anything these days."

"Think it over. If you like I'll talk to him about it for you."

"This is on the level, Carl?"

"I said it was. I'm interested in the gang he's kicking around with."

"Why?"

"A girl named Betty Brandt got knocked off this morning. The cops are trying to tag me with it. I need information and I need it bad."

"Betty Brandt?" Dolly looked surprised. "Redhead? Kind of skinny?"

"Redheaded but not exactly skinny," I said. "Know her?"

"If she's the one I think, she's one of Roy Green's girls."

"Roy's dead, too."

Dolly's eyes bulged a little. "Honest to God? You mean he got knocked off, too?"

"Knife." I moved a finger across my throat. "Some time this morning. The heat may not know about it yet."

"How'd you find out?"

"I stumbled over the body. I figured Roy was pushing dope."

"Not Roy." Dolly shook her head. "He was too smart to get tangled in anything like that. He had a nice school of fillies lined up and according to what I heard last, he was doing okay. Betty worked for me a while, but just about the time I got her established, she went independent. I could have put the screws to her, but I didn't, figuring she'd see the light and come back eventually. Then I heard she'd tied in with Roy and that he'd given her quite a set-up." Dolly paused and moistened her lips. "Did she get knifed, too?"

"No."

"Someone put a bullet in her, huh?"

"She got strangled."

"How terrible!" Dolly shivered realistically, making her heavy body quiver like jello which had suddenly contracted malaria. "She was sort of a nice kid. You think somebody in the troupe killed her?"

"I doubt it."

"What's your pitch, then, Carl? I don't get it."

"I'm scurrying around, asking questions, trying to raise a little dust, Dolly. You know how us private eyes work. We snoop around, asking a lot of questions and annoying people, then Lady Luck smiles and we pick up a couple bucks.

TOO YOUNG TO DIE

Betty Brandt was friendly with one of the girls in the troupe. For all I know, she may have been friendly with some of the guys, too. If she was a looker, it's more than likely. I want to locate them and find out what the hell's going on, before the cops jump all over me again."

Dolly digested this a moment, then she pushed back her chair. "Okay, boy. I'll see what I can do. Sit tight." She squeezed among the tables to the door and went upstairs.

The jukebox began blaring *I Cry For You* and the chorus at the bar, swaying as one, earnestly watered their beers with sentimental tears. I sipped my scotch and pondered the few bits of information I'd gleaned. Betty Brandt had been operating as a lady of the evening. Roy Greene had been peddling flesh, not dope. It was a tenuous link between the two killings, but it didn't explain much. A high-priced girl is a valuable property and a highly respected commodity in the rackets. Such women are traded, stolen, annexed, beaten up, and sometimes confiscated—but rarely killed because demand for their wares is great and replacement difficult. If Betty Brandt had been on Roy Greene's string and someone wanted her, the logical procedure would be to kill Greene and grab the girl, simply telling her that the management had changed.

But Greene *and* the girl had been killed. Either someone had blundered badly or the Brandt kid had been so intimately involved with the killing of Greene that her death had been dictated by the principle of self-preservation. But she had been killed first, hadn't she? If so, her death had been a necessary preliminary to Greene's. And the packet of morphine had to be sketched into the picture. Perhaps she had passed it to Greene, thereby double-dealing someone else; perhaps their victim had caught the play and had wrung her neck for it.

But, then, who had killed Greene? And why the elaborate

78

set-up? And if the dope was the motivation, why hadn't the killer grabbed it?

I was still pushing the pieces around in my mind like an idiot playing scrabble—and with about the same results— when Dolly returned. Her face was flushed and, judging by the nervous way in which her bosom was heaving, she'd reached for an apple and touched a snake.

"The cops found Roy!" she announced in an explosive gasp. "They've got a pick-up order out for you!"

Seven

Sweet and Deadly

I SWORE SOFTLY.

"They've got it on Ed Roberts' news round-up," Dolly went on excitedly. "He says the cops suspect you of having been on the scene when Roy was killed. Were you?"

"The whole set-up is a frame, Dolly. They're trying to push it down over my ears and onto my neck. I didn't think the cops would get on it this fast, though. Somebody must have tipped them."

"I know a good spot where you can duck, Carl. A friend of mine's got a place—"

"Thanks, but I've got to keep moving. Did you locate Red Dog?"

"No, but Ciggie Price, who usually knows what's going on, says that Ed Zike's in town and that Ed's got a girl and a couple of guys working with him. Ed used to be a pretty good wire, you know, and he's been out of Statesville now more than six months. It's the only troupe Ciggie knows about."

"Sounds likely," I said, nodding slowly. "Where can I locate Zike?"

"Ciggie says Zike's working out of a kitchenette on Huron

Street. He didn't know the number, but it's a big white frame building on the north side of the street, just east of State Street."

"I'll spot it. One more thing—"

"What?"

"There's probably a squad or two cruising the street. How about flagging a cab and having it pick me up in the alley?"

"That's easy." She rose. "You won't forget to put in a word for me with Red Dog?"

"You can count on it, Dolly. I never forget my friends."

She made a confident circle with thumb and forefinger. "I'll get the cab. Good luck, Carl."

She moved away, forcing her bulky body between chairs and elbowing a path among clumps of swaying singers. I waited until she reached the front door, then pushed back my chair. I'd used the rear entrance on previous occasions and had no difficulty locating it. A truck loaded with empty soda bottles was stalled at one end of the alley; the other exit was clear and deserted. I closed the door and took a deep breath. The stench of ancient beer and decaying food filled my nostrils. In self-defense, I lit a cigarette and flicked the match at a nearby garbage can. A cloud of flies rose, droning angrily, and the stench became more acute. Jetting smoke from my nostrils, I moved away from the garbage, keeping close to the buildings.

A blue Vet Cab pointed its nose into the alley, its thin-faced driver leaning out to give me the high-sign. I spun my cigarette away and ran toward the cab. He smiled tightly, letting me get a glimpse of a scarred cheek, and opened the rear door. I dove in and banged it shut. He shifted the gears without instructions from me and executed a deft back and turn.

"Dolly said you were hot," he commented dryly. "Where you headed?"

"Cruise around to Huron Street," I said. "Let me know if you spot any heat."

"East or west?"

"East. Take it slow."

"Don't worry, I been on the lam myself a couple times. What they trying to get you for?"

"The big sting."

"No kidding." A note of respect tinged his voice and I felt his interest quicken. "Dolly said you were okay, but she didn't tell me the pitch."

"Get me to State and Huron without being spotted and I'll be grateful."

"Cinch." He cut over to Dearborn, went north to Huron, then headed toward State. "Which building?"

"The big white one on the left. Get as close to it as you can."

"Natch." He swerved the cab suddenly and leaped across the street and plunged into a narrow driveway beside the big frame building. "How's this?" he asked, grinding to a stop.

"Fine." I dropped a couple bills onto the seat beside him.

"Want me to wait?"

I thought a moment. Square cabbies are few and far between, and this one had been picked by Dolly, which meant that he had a good rep and could be trusted. "I might be inside quite a while," I said.

He smiled crookedly. "I done three years of waiting, not so long ago, the hard way."

"Okay," I said. "Better park down the street a ways, in case I'm spotted."

"Don't worry about me. Think you might be coming out in a hurry?"

"I doubt it."

"If you do, I'll be ready." He gunned the cab back, turned

it swiftly, and aimed at a parking spot near the corner. I went up four steps to a porch, opened an unlatched screen door, and stepped into a small old-fashioned lobby, complete with potted rubber-plants and throw-rugs. A sanctimonious-looking old clerk in a sweat-spotted shirt pulled his nose away from an open ledger and eyed me wearily.

"Ed Zike," I said briskly. "Know if he's in?"

"Haven't any idea," he admitted, wheezing asthmatically. "Probably ain't." He lifted an eyebrow. "Want me to buzz him?"

"I'll go on up."

"Sure." He held a gnarled hand in front of his lips and wheezed delicately, then sneezed. "Take the stairs," he managed to gasp, motioning with one hand. "Third floor. Apartment D."

The stairs went up and around in a jerky zigzag like an old maid's stockings. I ascended them hurriedly, getting only a whisper of protest from the faded carpeting. At the third floor, the stairs ended abruptly and I found myself in a yellow-and-green painted corridor which ran the length of the building. The air smelled faintly of long-dead cigars, cheaply perfumed women and fairly recent bacon grease.

Behind the thin panel of apartment B, pans and dishes were rattling busily and the unctuous voice of a sponsor-conscious radio announcer was proudly proclaiming something about Duz doing everything. Apartment C was as silent as a pair of lovers under a tree. I paused momentarily at D, then walked past and scouted the area beyond. There were two apartments, both with closed doors. E betrayed no sounds of occupancy, but in F a high, tinkly voice, reminding me of brittle tea cups clinking in a sink, was spieling breathlessly and continuously. I listened a moment and gathered that she and Billie had had lunch at Stouffer's and the creamed corned beef had been divine. Since I could hear no answering cries of envy or ecstacy, I decided that the apartment contained a feather-brained woman glued to a phone. Satisfied, I walked back to D and tapped my fingers against the door.

The panel reverberated hollowly. I waited and listened, then tapped again, a little louder this time. There was no answering patter of feet within, no sound of movement at all. I deliberated briefly, studying the flimsy construction of the door and the placement of the spring lock which held it closed. Temptation won. With a flat key, I pried up the wooden molding along the side of the door and inserted the thin edge of a celluloid card-window from my wallet. The lock sprung open easily and the door opened.

I hammered the molding back into place with my hand and stepped into the apartment, closing the door firmly behind me.

It was a standard big-city cubicle, a testimony to the purse-conscious taste of a landlord. The bed, dresser and chairs were of maple, cheap but substantial. A checkerboard of black and white linoleum covered the floor. Two rural scenes in cheap frames hung against the painted plywood walls. The covering of the bed was rumpled and soiled, showing clearly where a body had lain and perspired. A plaid sportcoat, once gay with color, drooped forlornly from a chair-back. To my left there was a tiny bathroom, to my right an even tinier stove-sink-and-icebox combination.

I examined the dresser first. It contained two shirts, a pair of new cotton socks, several handkerchiefs, and a sparse assortment of cheap undershirts and shorts. These had been tossed carelessly into the top drawer. The other two drawers were empty. I walked to a closet. Except for a pair of brown gabardine slacks which hung from a wire hanger, the closet was bare. Zike, apparently, was a man of few worldly possessions.

THE FLESH PEDDLERS

I checked the bathroom. Besides the usual equipment, there was a cheap safety razor, a bar of hotel-size soap, a tube of toothpaste, a stiff-bristled toothbrush, and several flimsy towels, all soiled and semi-damp. I lifted the lid of the water-closet and peered in, thinking he might have read a book about where to hide things. He hadn't.

The icebox contained two cans of beer, a dish of baked beans and three shriveled weiners. Zike was no cook. I studied the stove, then got down on my knees and stared at the dirt-filmed bottom of the sink. Feeling somewhat frustrated, I turned my attention to the bed. The mattress was thin and lumpy; I prodded it in all the likely places, but the lumps were legitimate in origin. I lifted it up and eyed the wire springs. Only a bedbug could hide there. I let the mattress flop back into place and pushed the covers around until they looked natural. Apparently Zike was smart enough not to stash anything in his flop.

I had a hand in the side-pocket of the sport jacket when I heard the rapid clatter of hurrying feet in the corridor. I took a deep breath and froze. The footsteps came down the corridor and stopped directly in front of the door. There was a metallic click, as of a purse being opened, then a faint jingle of keys. I jerked my fingers out of the jacket pocket as though it had snapped at me and retreated swiftly into the closet.

The apartment door opened and closed, then footsteps crossed the room rapidly. I crouched in the dark closet and peered through the narrow slit which I'd left open.

For my purposes, the closet was poorly located. My field of vision was restricted to a few feet of space in front of the gas plate and, to take in even that much, I had to weave my head from side to side in a short arc. The footsteps stopped near where I judged the bed to be, remained silent for several seconds, then recrossed the room in a different direction. There was silence for a while, then I heard the toilet flush. Immediately, the footsteps returned, paused indecisively, then began to move about in a confusingly aimless manner, as though pacing the floor.

I strained my eyes against the crack and kept my head moving from side to side like a well-oiled oscillating fan. At last a slim nylon-clad leg and a high-heeled black pump flicked past the crack, vanishing instantly as the pacing continued.

I sighed inwardly and tried to ease my aching leg muscles. The footsteps stopped suddenly and the bedsprings squeaked a faint protest. With infinite care I braced my arms against the inner jamb of the door frame and shifted my weight. When she reappeared, it was so silently and swiftly that I nearly missed her. She bent over the sink, showing me a slice of blue skirt, a nicely curved posterior and a long, shoeless leg. Water splashed and a glass clinked, then she turned away and disappeared again. But in the brief instant that she was directly in front of the crack, I had glimpsed short curly blonde hair and a familiar blouse.

Things clicked in my head: Zike's visitor was Tina Rogers, the blonde kid I'd seen beating a hasty retreat from Betty Brandt's apartment . . .

For what seemed an eternity, there was no sound in the room except the muted sibilance of my own breathing. Then a match flared and the bedsprings did a creaky glissando. I shifted my weight again. She reappeared suddenly, minus skirt and blouse, to give me a slick lingerie-ad view of a youthful, voluptuous figure clad in bra, half-slip, and gartered nylons. With what seemed like vehemence, she moistened a comb at the sink and raked it through her hair. She repeated the gesture several times, accomplishing no visible improvement, then flung the comb aside. A gentleman would have coughed discreetly or closed his eyes at this point. I

86

pursed my lips judiciously and, while she dabbed at her neck and armpits with a wet cloth, I tried to control my red corpuscles by attempting a scientific estimate of her age and antecedents. She came from muscular, fertile, well-built stock, I decided, and she was a kid. She was twenty, maybe less. She had nice hips, a good pelvis. It would be easy for her to have children.

I must have been absorbed in my study, for I didn't hear the door of the apartment open. She uttered a subdued cry of alarm suddenly and spun half-around, flinging an arm across her breasts.

"Ed!" she cried in an outraged contralto. "Where the hell have you been?"

"Hello, honey." It was a smooth voice, unsurprised and not really interested.

The blonde snatched the bra from the sink, plunged into it expertly, then moved away from the crack. "You've got a hell of a lot of nerve," she said angrily. "You said you'd meet me after the caper."

"How'd you get in here?"

"With a key, of course."

"So that's where it went." Zike's voice betrayed mild astonishment. "You're getting pretty good, Tina. Maybe instead of spotting and stalling, you should work a few fobs or try your hand at the hangers."

"I'm not buying any of that, Ed. Don't try to change the subject. You said you'd meet me. Why didn't you?"

"I got delayed."

"Where?"

"None of your business. I told you there weren't to be any strings on me, and I meant it."

"Don't be a fool, Ed. I don't give a damn about you personally. I'm talking about my split. Catch on? You said you'd meet me right after the caper."

"I haven't got it from Samp yet."

"Like hell."

"That's the truth, Tina. I don't know what happened to him. That's why I didn't show. I've been chasing around, trying to figure his play. Red Dog's plenty sore."

"So am I. I need the dough. I told you that this morning."

"You don't need it any worse than I do. Look at this dump." The bedsprings creaked and squirmed. "I had a better flop than this when I was in the can."

"You're going to wish you were back in the can if I don't get my split." Tina's voice sharpened warningly. "I told you I had to have it. I need it bad."

"What do you need it for?"

"What do you care?"

"You thinking of ditching the troupe?"

"It wouldn't be the first time."

"Tina, make sense."

"I'm making sense. You're too dumb to understand it."

"Look, kid. When I ran into you, you were peddling magazines and making peanuts. You hadn't gone on the make yet, but you were dragging your tail and you know damned well that in a couple days you'd have been walking the streets and shaking your can like the other two-bit floosies on Division Street. But I gave you a break. I got you some decent clothes and I showed you the ins and outs of a better racket. Now, just when I develop some grift sense in you and we start binging them pretty good, you got to get temperamental like a goddam prima donna. With Red Dog fingering for us, we've got the sharpest set-up in the country. Inside of a couple weeks, we'll be knocking suckers off like they were paralyzed. I told you that's the way it was going to be, and the job we did this morning was a sample. It couldn't have gone any smoother. Red Dog said the sucker had a big roll

—and Samp's got it. The troupe's working out. We've got a perfect set-up."

"Like hell." Tina's tone was scornful. "You said the jug was a cinch and that we'd each get a couple C's—"

"It *was* a cinch. It worked out just like I said it would—"

"Then where's the dough?"

"Samp's got it. I told you that when—"

"Sure, *Samp's* got it!" She spat the sentence. "You'd think Samp was a girl the way you've been babying him. I happen to know that all the time you were crying the blues to me, you were slipping dough to him!"

"Hell, Tina, I had to. Samp's a good cannon, and you know he couldn't work without a fix. I had to keep him in condition, didn't I?"

"Then how about keeping me in condition? I need a hundred bucks right now!"

"There's less than a tenner in my pocket, Tina. That's God's truth."

"You're lying!"

"I'm not. It cost me dough to get Red Dog here, and everybody's had to eat and, like I said, Samp's had to have—"

"You're giving me a run-around. You met Samp and collected the take. If you think you can play me for a sucker, Ed Zike, you'd better think again. Either I get my dough or—"

"Or what?" Zike interrupted scornfully. "I don't have to give you a damned dime. I'm running this troupe. I could kick you out, and you could scream until you're blue in the face, and all the cops will give you is a big laugh."

"Any screaming I do, it won't be to the cops!"

"Yeah, yeah, I know. You're giving me a headache."

"And what do you think you're giving me?" She flung the question at him and her voice rose dangerously.

"I'm not giving you a damned thing."

"You're giving me my dough!"

"Like hell."

"You admit you've got it, then!"

"I'm not admitting a damned thing. You can just shake your tail out of here and—" There was a sharp crack, like that of a dry lath snapping. Zike's voice paused, then, somewhat surprised, said: "Why, you little bitch! Just for that, I'll—"

The crack was repeated, then Tina squealed with fury and I caught the sound of scuffling. I touched the door with my fingertips and pushed it open a bit. I heard Zike curse softly and caught the flash of a thrashing nylon-sheathed leg, but the door blocked my view. I opened it farther. Tina, clad in a rosy flush of fury from the waist up, had her hands locked in Zike's hair and was earnestly trying to pull him off the bed. Zike, cursing fluently, rolled off the bed and gained his feet. He struck at her arms, then kneed her viciously. She let go his hair, raking her nails across his face. Zike flung a fist at her face, missed, and tried to rush her. With a frightened whimper, she sprang away, tripped against a chair and went sprawling on the floor. She landed hard but rolled like a kitten and ended up smack beside the high-heeled pumps which she'd kicked off earlier.

Zike saw his danger and with a hoarse cry he dove for her. He landed across her heaving chest, knocking some of the breath from her lungs, but his hands missed the fingers which now clutched a high-heeled pump.

"Tina—!" he gasped.

"You stinker." She said it emotionlessly and brought the shoe down twice, hard and deliberate like a carpenter driving in a nail. Zike crumpled suddenly, lying half across her. She eyed him suspiciously for a moment, then pushed him away and got to her feet. Still clutching the shoe, she stood spread-legged beside him, eyes watchful and distrusting. Zike lay

90

motionless, but he appeared to be breathing. She bent down, began to examine the pockets of his trousers. Zike moaned faintly. She stood up holding a wallet. She opened it quickly, then blew through her lips disgustedly and flung it across the room. Zike moaned again and made moist bubbling sounds with his lips. Her face hardened and, stalking around to where his head lay, she raised the shoe and hammered him again behind the ear.

She was arcing the shoe for a second blow when I stepped out of the closet and wrapped an arm around her neck.

Eight

Charity Begins

SHE STIFFENED FOR AN instant, as though frozen by my touch. Then she twisted violently like a frightened animal. I tightened my arm cruelly, forcing her chin up and back, and slapped my other arm across her writhing belly. Her skin was hot and slippery. She kept twisting with the eccentric movement and strength of a desperate cat. I got a firm grip and dug my fingers into her side, pulling her against me so tightly that I could feel her muscles rippling against my shirt like a bag full of snakes.

"Drop the shoe," I growled into her ear.

She tensed, as though gathering strength for a final attempt at escape, then the fight went out of her. She relaxed in my arms and the shoe clumped to the floor. I kicked it across the room.

"Going to behave?" I asked.

Her neck jerked meekly and a strangled cry struggled past my arm. I loosened my hold gradually, then stepped away from her. She turned and eyed me sullenly, massaging the front of her throat with one hand and attempting to straighten her twisted skirt with the other. Her face was flushed, and, the way her thick blonde hair was tousled and her high young breasts were heaving, she looked like a ravished nymph.

"Get dressed," I said. "You're giving me sore eyes."

The flush deepened. With a whipped look on her pretty face, she crossed the room and began struggling into her clothes. I knelt beside Zike and laid a hand on his chest. He was breathing. I sighed my relief and got to my feet. She had part of her clothes on and was staring at the open door of the closet.

"Hurry up," I said. "Zike isn't dead, but somebody may have called the cops. We've got to get out of here."

She nodded and began poking her arms into the blouse. I collected her shoes and dropped them in front of her. She buttoned the blouse, wriggled her feet into the black pumps, then began raking at her hair.

"You can primp later," I snapped impatiently. "This way, sister."

Taking her by the arm, I pulled her toward the door. She came meekly enough, but I knew that her thinking apparatus had resumed functioning and that she was doing some rapid mental addition. Before she could get too many of the right sums, I rushed her downstairs. The clerk was nodding over his ledger. As we emerged from the building, the blue Vet Cab roared to life and started toward us. I led her to the curb, keeping a tight grip on her arm. The cabbie, betraying no surprise, ground to a stop and flung open the rear door. She started to get in, then stopped as if suddenly alarmed and began backing out. I slapped her where her skirt was tightest. She sucked in her breath sharply, jerked her hips violently, and bounced onto the seat. I climbed in after her and slammed the door.

"Head north," I told the driver.

He nodded knowingly and got the cab rolling. I sat sidewise on the seat so I could look at her. She was sitting stif-

fly erect, as though the back of the seat were studded with
nails, and her chin was poked out in a hard, defiant line, but
her hands were nested in her lap like a bunch of pale, frightened worms and her eyes were suspiciously moist around the
edges.

"Where do you live, Tina?" I asked.

A muscle in her throat quivered. "Who," she demanded,
"wants to know?"

"You may not realize it, but I'm doing you a favor," I
said. "You could have killed Zike."

A flame licked at the darkness behind her eyes. "He needs
killing," she said bitterly. "I'm sorry you stopped me."

"Don't be a fool. Murder draws a rough jolt."

"So does kidnaping!"

"You don't act much like a kid."

That stung her a little, but she tossed her head and stared
straight ahead. The cab had turned north on Dearborn
Street and was heading for Lincoln Park. Silence thickened
between us for several blocks, then she jerked her head
around abruptly and asked. "Where are you taking me?"

"Ottawa Arms."

Her eyes went wide in sudden consternation. "W-why?"

"I thought you might like another peek at Betty Brandt."

"W-who are you?" The tremble in her voice was genuine; so was the stark horror in her eyes.

"My name is Good. Carl Good. I'm a private cop. I saw
you high-tail it out of Betty's apartment right after she was
killed."

"Oh!" The syllable was pregnant with sudden recollection.
"Y-you're the man who got in the elevator, the one the cops
were looking for!"

"Sure." I grinned. "As a matter of fact, they're still looking for me. We're both sort of on the run. But you're going
at things bass-ackwards. Zike couldn't split with you because

he didn't get the loot. I think Samp ducked with it."

"The lousy creep!" Anger brightened the blue of her eyes. "If I ever get my hands on him—!"

"Use your head, Tina. There's been enough violence. I'm anxious to locate Samp, but I want him in one piece. What's his real name?"

She stared at me a moment. "What's in this for me?" she asked.

"A clean sheet with the cops," I said. "You may need a witness to prove you didn't kill Betty. I was right on your heels and can swear you weren't in her apartment long enough to do anything except look and run."

She bit her lip.

"Also," I said, "I'm on Samp's trail. I can't promise anything definite but, if I locate him, it might do you some good."

She was still reluctant, still not completely sold, but the initial sullenness and fear had drained out of her and I had the feeling that, when she made up her mind, it would be in my favor. The fact that I talked her language probably tipped the scales and got me the decision.

She moistened her lips. "His name is Paul," she said. "Paul Constantine."

"Where is he staying?"

"Wherever he can bum a bed or a fix."

"Has he been bunking with Betty?"

"How would I know?" she flared.

"She was a friend of yours, wasn't she?"

"I don't know." She jerked her shoulders with exaggerated unconcern. "I knew her, sort of, but only because she was trying to get me to switch rackets. I wouldn't say she was a friend."

"What kind of a racket was she plugging, Tina?"

"A charity deal. She didn't give me any details, but she

95

said there was dough in it for a girl who could think on her feet. She knew that I was getting fed up with Zike's promises and had about made up my mind to quit the troupe. So she started selling me on this other racket and promised to fix things for me as soon as I got some decent clothes and . . . well, you know. I had to look like something besides a kid fresh from the country."

"That's why you're so anxious for the dough?"

"Of course."

"She didn't explain her racket?"

"No, she just said it was hardly any work at all and that I could make maybe a hundred dollars a day once I got started. I know she made that much, at least; she used to throw money around like it was confetti. Once, she—"

"Heat coming!" the cab driver warned abruptly. "Better duck!" I slid off the seat onto the floor of the cab and bent my head down between my knees. A car swished past. "Okay," the driver said tonelessly.

"Thanks." I climbed back onto the seat. "I don't want to be ducking every five minutes. Can you find a quiet place to park?"

"How about around the back of the greenhouses?"

"Good enough."

He circled expertly and nosed the cab into a space beside a huge glass-paned building. "How long you going to be talking?" he asked.

"Long enough for you to look at the tulips."

"That's what I figured." He climbed out slowly. "Blow the horn if you need me." Limping slightly, he crossed a patch of grass and went toward a curving bed of bright-red tulips.

"We were talking about Betty Brandt," I said. "Who do you think killed her?"

"I don't know. Honest."

"Samp, maybe?"

96

"He wouldn't have had the guts."

"A junkie doesn't need guts. He went into the building quite a while before you did. He had time to kill her. Was Betty hitting the needle?"

"Not that I know of."

"Samp didn't live in the Ottawa Arms, did he?"

"I told you he didn't."

"When you ran out of Betty's apartment, where did you duck?"

"I . . . I went to another apartment."

"Which one?"

"Five-thirty-five."

"Whose apartment is that?"

"Mine."

I stared at her. "You were supposed to rendezvous with the others, but you headed for the Ottawa Arms and went straight to Betty's apartment instead of your own? Why?"

"I went to the rendezvous, but only Red Dog was there. None of the others had showed yet. So I told Red Dog to stay there, and I took a cab back to the apartment intending to change clothes. Then, I got to thinking about Betty's proposition, and I decided to stop and tell her that I was ready to throw in with her. You see, Red Dog told me that the wallet Samp lifted was loaded with big bills, and I figured that my cut would give me enough to buy all the clothes Betty said I'd have to have. Her door was open and . . . and I just walked in and found her."

"How long did you know Betty?"

"A couple of weeks. I saw her in the lobby several times, and then we rode up in the elevator together and started talking. She asked me to come in and have a drink with her."

"Did you talk to her last night?"

"No. She was usually out in the evening. We talked for about ten minutes yesterday afternoon, though."

"Did she seem worried or upset or nervous about anything?"

"Gosh, no! She'd just been to Saks to look at some evening gowns and she kept describing the three she'd ordered. I'd never seen her so gay or excited."

"Did she mention who was paying for them?"

"Why . . . she was paying for them, of course!"

"Did she say so?"

"No, but—"

"So she could have put the bite on some guy for them, for all you know. Did she ever mention the men in her life?"

Tina shook her head slowly. "No. I hadn't thought of it before, but . . . I don't think she had any steady boy friends. She didn't exactly say so, but I got the impression that she didn't like or trust men."

"Did she make any passes at you?"

Her cheeks flushed the color of a sun-ripened plum. "Don't get smart. I didn't mean it that way, and you know it. She went out with men. She wasn't that kind of wrongo. But a couple times she made remarks that . . . well, that were kind of bitter, as though she'd been burnt and wasn't taking any more chances."

"She's been burnt plenty," I said flatly.

"How do you know?"

"She was a party girl, working the guys with fat pockets for all she could get."

"Oh, no!"

"Oh, yes," I mimicked dryly. "You don't think she made a hundred bucks a day shaking that tin canister, do you? The charity angle was probably a front. Once you spent all your dough for clothes, and were desperate, she'd have broken the news to you. Did you ever see a solicitor for the Salvation Army decked out in fancy evening clothes?"

"I can't believe it!" She looked as though she'd swallowed

a putrid oyster. "Betty was always so . . . so sympathetic!"

"Sure," I agreed. "Pawnbrokers are sympathetic, too, but it's a front; they screw every dime they can out of you. If Betty got you lined up, she'd have collected a bonus from somebody higher up. You're a grown girl and you're in a big city, so stop being so naive."

"But . . ."

"Facts are facts, Tina. For a while Betty worked out of a place a friend of mine used to run, then she teamed up with a peddler named Roy Greene, then she went independent. The charity gimmick suggests that maybe she threw in with some new organization. But no matter what the set-up, she was selling the oldest commodity known to man and doing pretty well at it. I guess someone didn't like the way she operated. Did she ever mention Roy Greene to you?"

"No."

"Hell." I spat the word disgustedly, for it was pretty obious that I was getting no place fast. Either Tina Rogers was as innocent as a freshly laid egg, or she was far more clever than I had thought.

"This . . . this Roy Greene. Is he important?" she asked suddenly.

"Not any more. Someone knocked him off."

"They killed him, too?"

"For chrissake, that's what I said, isn't it?" I snapped irritably. She recoiled as though I'd slapped her. Ignoring her, I switched to a different line of attack. "How well did Samp know Betty Brandt?"

"How would I know?" she snapped back, sounding as though I'd accused her of peeking under bedroom shades.

"You knew them both. You'd know if he'd been hanging around her, wouldn't you?"

"He dropped in once or twice while I was with her. There

wasn't anything between them. They were . . . well, different types."

"He was a guy, she was a girl. Sometimes it helps when people are different."

"No. Not Samp and Betty."

"Then who else did Samp know in the building?"

"Nobody that I know of."

"He made a bee-line there from the bank, so he was headed either for your apartment or Betty's. Did he have a key to your apartment?"

"You've got a hell of a lot of nerve—" she began.

"Look, Tina," I cut in, "there isn't time for a lot of tactful sparring. He's a man and you're a woman, and anything is possible. All you have to do is give me a simple answer: did he or didn't he have a key to your place?"

"He didn't."

"Do you think he had a key to Betty's apartment?"

"No."

"Why not?"

"Betty wasn't that kind of a girl."

"She was for sale, like I told you."

"I mean, Betty wouldn't give a key to a man unless he was paying the rent—and Samp wasn't; he was broke."

I thought that over a moment.

"He could have lifted one from her, couldn't he?"

"I suppose." She shrugged. "He has a pretty slick dip."

"Then Samp could have gone to Betty's apartment, gotten in with a key, and surprised her as she was dressing."

Tina shook her head. "I don't think so."

"Why not?"

"There's a chain on her door. She always kept it latched. Whenever I went to see her, she'd open the door a few inches, peek out, then close it so she could release the chain. Samp couldn't have gotten in without her doing that."

"So she wasn't surpirsed. Whoever killed her was someone she knew intimately and trusted." I thought of the dead girl as I had seen her, freshly bathed and half-naked and looking as though she had been flung onto the bed. "How about Betty's girl friends?" I asked. "Who did she pal around with?"

"She never said. The only girl she ever mentioned was one named Lucy."

"Lucy who?"

"I never heard the rest of her name, just Lucy. I think she double-dated with Betty occasionally. Or maybe they worked together. I'm not sure."

"Did you ever see her?"

"No."

"Damn." Apparently I was stalemated. I'd wasted a lot of precious time trying to dig information out of the blonde, and she knew even less than I did. My troubles pivoted on the killing of Roy Greene, and the link between Greene and Betty Brandt was the fact that she had once been on his string. Question: What had been Betty Brandt's current tie-up? Question: Where had Samp disappeared to? Question: Whose side was Patricia Greene on? Most important: Who was engineering the frame?

"Mr. Good—?" Her voice, faintly troubled, worked through the gloom clogging my mind. "Mr. Good—?"

"Yeah."

"Why are you troubling yourself about . . . about these things?"

"Somebody's trying to frame me for the killing of Roy Greene."

"Did you?"

"Did I what?"

"Did you kill him?"

"Hell, no. I didn't even know the jerk."

101

"But I don't see—"

"It's complicated, Tina, very complicated." More for my own instruction than hers, I went over the salient points of the mess, trying to fit the jagged pieces into some semblance of a whole. It made less sense than ever.

When I finished, her lips were parted and she was staring at me with horrified concern. "But that's . . . *that's dirty!*" she cried. "Whoever's doing this is a sneaky rouster type!"

"He's worse than that; he's a killer," I said grimly.

"Would it help you any if you knew who Betty was . . . working for?"

"It might."

She bit her lip. "She made me promise never to tell anyone."

"That was before she knew that she was going to get killed."

Her eyes widened with horror. "You mean . . . you mean Betty knew that . . . that she was being killed?"

I nodded. "Probably. She was strangled, and usually there are several seconds of consciousness before the big black wraps things up. She knew what was happening, all right."

"How horrible!"

"It wasn't pleasant. You saw her. She didn't look as though she'd enjoyed it, did she?"

"No." She shuddered suddenly. "Look, I guess I ought to level with you. For Betty's sake. She meant well, and . . . well, you sound like a right guy." She moistened her red lips and looked into my eyes. "What I told you before wasn't entirely true. I knew she'd been going out on calls. I figured it right away and, when I asked her about it, she admitted she'd been peddling. But she said the outfit she was working with had figured out a sleek way of doing things, and there wasn't anything the cops could do about it because the girls never actually accepted any money."

"If the girls didn't, who did?"

"It went into one of those little round cans like all the charity organizations use, and the girls took them to a real office, just like it was a legitimate contribution which they'd collected, and the doctor there opened the cans and gave them their split in cash. Betty said her end of the deal was a straight fifty per cent."

"A doctor?" I echoed sharply.

"Sure. That's what made it a sweet set-up, she said. The cops were afraid to tangle with the Brotherhood."

"The Brotherhood?" I was beginning to sound like a parrot.

"That's what it's called . . . The Brotherhood for Service. It even sounds legitimate, doesn't it?"

"Did she mention the doctor's name?"

"Sure. Doctor Greene."

"Greene!" I stiffened. *"Roy Greene was a doctor?"*

"Not a medical doctor. Just a title, see? And I told you I didn't know any Roy Greene. Anyway, this doctor is a woman. I don't know her first name. Betty usually just called her Doctor Greene. Sort of mocking like. You know."

"I can imagine," I said dryly. The idea of a female doctor steering a line of play girls bombed my mind, crowding other speculations into dark corners. If it worked the way Tina said, the set-up was terrific—and so was the payoff. Doctor Greene, whoever she was, was undoubtedly splitting the take at least three ways: A hunk to the Brotherhood, a big hunk for herself, and an even bigger hunk to the cops. Inevitably, other eyes would watch the juicy take, and other hands would itch for a slice of it. Suddenly a vision of Patricia Greene with her black hair and thin, ascetic face leaped across my mind and I felt the soft fur of a sapphire mink jacket brushing against my fingertips. Doctor Greene.

Patricia Greene. Mrs. Roy Greene. In a crazy, mixed-up way, it figured.

I leaned over the back of the front seat and rammed my hand against the horn button. The horn squawked like a frightened duck. The cabbie came running.

Nine

Sing And Slug

"A TELEPHONE," I SAID as he flung himself behind the wheel. He nodded, kicked at the starter and got the cab into reverse. A moment later we were barreling out of the park. He executed a jolting stop across the street from the Commonwealth Drugstore on Diversey. "Sit tight," I told him. "I'll only be a minute."

Morrie Tannen answered his phone on the second ring.

"This is Carl," I said. "Anything doing?"

"A couple of bulls were in," he said cautiously. "You're pretty hot."

"I heard. Did you make those calls?"

"Yes." He cleared his throat.

"Well?"

"Greene's clean. He wasn't peddling."

I frowned. "The hell he wasn't. Who'd you ask?"

"Several men who ought to know. The word is that he handled flesh, not dope."

"Okay, Morrie. Thanks." I tried to keep the disappointment out of my voice.

"Anything else I can do?"

"You might dust off a couple *habeas corpus* forms, just in

case. Incidentally, did you ever hear of the Brotherhood for Service?"

"No."

"It's a girl operation piloted by a female phony doctor named Greene. I have a hunch she was Roy Greene's wife. It might help if I knew who the fix is."

"I'll ask, Carl. Are you making progress?"

"Like a snail," I told him. "I'll call you later tonight."

I hung up quickly and trotted back to the cab. Tina, looking somewhat guilty, tossed her head pettishly and sank back in the seat as I climbed in. "She wanted to duck while you were in there," the driver announced in a monotone. "I told her I'd heave a wrench across her neck."

"So why shouldn't I go?" the blonde demanded. "I've told you everything I know. You don't need me any more."

"You're right, Tina," I agreed. "Thanks a lot. You can get out here if you like."

Her chin dropped an inch. "You mean you want to get rid of me?"

"Of course not." I grinned. "You said you've told me everything you know, and I believe you. I don't want to inconvenience you any more than necessary."

"But . . . but I could cry cop." There was puzzlement in her voice.

"You'd be cutting off your own nose."

"Why?"

"The killer may think you know more than you do."

"Oh." She blinked. "You mean *I'm* in danger?"

"Probably not," I admitted. "It's a possibility though."

"But . . . there isn't anything else I can do, is there?"

"Not unless you felt like sticking your neck out."

"How?"

"You might try to contact the Doctor. Tell her you're new in the city, need dough, and that you heard she was looking

106

for fresh talent. With Betty out of circulation permanently, she'll be looking for a replacement and you're young and pretty enough to get serious attention."

"But I haven't the clothes for—"

"Clothes can be bought or borrowed. If she feels you have possibilities, she'd stake you to the dough. It would be a good investment, from her point of view. Even if she turned you down, you'd have a chance to look around and maybe hear some inside dope on why Betty got killed."

"You think she'd turn me down?" Her voice rose subtly.

"No, I don't. You're young and pretty. Girls like you are in demand."

"Then you *want* me to become a—a bad girl?" Her nostrils flared a little.

"I didn't say that. It's your life and you can do as you damned please with it. I *did* say that it would help if you contacted the Doctor and tried to pick up some inside information."

"But you said I should ask for a job! What if—"

"Forget it," I said wearily. "It was simply an idea, a lousy idea. There wouldn't be a damned thing in it for you, either, unless you wanted to take over Betty's clientele, and apparently you've got scruples. Like a lot of kids, who have seen a lot of movies, you've probably been getting a kick out of imagining yourself living a life of sin—but when it comes time to lay things on the line, you remember the way mother used to whisper to you under the family magnolia tree—and the hell with Evil. As a matter of fact, I'm glad it's like that. Not all girls are that lucky. You look like a sweet kid, even though you've been running around with a pack of petty racketeers. I advise you to go back to Little Rock or West Bend or wherever you came from before you get picked up for consorting with a wanted man." I leaned over and opened the door. "Thanks, Tina. Maybe I'll see you around."

"All right." There was a definite fringe of icicles on the words. She got out slowly, like a girl who is afraid she'll snag her last pair of nylons. "Goodbye, Mr. Good!" She slammed the door, wheeled, and strode off, clicking her heels on the sidewalk as though trying to punch holes in the concrete.

"Women!" the cabbie commented, rolling the word on his tongue as though it tasted bitter.

"Some of them," I agreed. "This one is okay. She'll grow up some day. Say, what's your name?"

"Mostly I'm called Bertie the Bing." He uttered the moniker with quiet pride, like a man mentioning that he used to wear three stripes in the U. S. Marines.

"Statesville?"

"Joliet. I did three years, but I'm off the hook now." He moved his shoulders restlessly—as though feeling again the yoke of prison on them. "You got any plans?"

I glanced at my watch. It was nearly seven o'clock and my stomach was making sounds like a cement mixer full of rocks. "Drop me some place where I can get a meal, Bertie, then we'll call it a trip."

"Sure thing."

He drove me to a small joint called the Pine Tree Grill, near Chestnut and Rush Streets, and casually pocketed the bill I tossed him. "Call Dolly if you need a quick lift," he suggested, making a good luck sign with stubby fingers. I nodded and strode into the grill. I spent a half-hour eating a steak dinner and chewing over the information I'd gleaned from Tina and Morrie. The only thing which made sense was the steak. I decided I'd better get back on the job before the cops got onto me. In a classified phonebook, under Organizations, I found a listing of the Brotherhood for Service. Its address was on North Wells Street, near Menomonee. I decided to walk the short distance, and I headed for it briskly, taking the less traveled side-streets and keeping a sharp watch for cruising squad cars.

Dusk was seeping between the ramshackle buildings of the Old Town section when I reached Menomonee Street, casting low-key shadows as a prelude to gloom. As I turned the corner onto Wells, the wheezing tones of an old pipe organ hit my ears. I stared in the direction of the labored tones and made out a black amplifier horn perched high above the sidewalk in front of a double-windowed frame storefront. As I started toward it, the organ faltered, gasped for breath, then struggled into the opening chords of a hymn, and a chorus of ragged but determined voices began plucking at the words of *Come Unto Me All Those Who Sin*. My lips twisted into an involuntary grin; the selection seemed uncannily appropriate.

As I approached the building, the cacophony of voices and organ became deafening. In the doorway, a tall, thin man in a rumpled brown suit loitered, his lips moving in unison with the raucous organ. When he saw me, he smiled hopefully, exuding his version of brotherhood, and extended one hand holding a printed tract. I returned the smile and accepted the tract, which asked, in bold type: "Are *You* Ready?" I folded the tract and pushed it into a pocket, studying the building as I did so.

It was the usual, stereotyped mission set-up, with one window containing a large open Bible on a miniature lectern and the other displaying the neon promise: JESUS SAVES. At the rear of the windows a black velvet drape hung, strung on taut wires, protecting the worshipers from the stares of passersby. Lettered on the door was: BROTH-ERHOOD FOR SERVICE. *P. L. Greene, Ph.D, D.D.* WEL-COME!

The voices rose triumphantly in a final invitation to sinners and the organ wheezed to an asthmatic conclusion. I

109

opened the door and stepped inside. It was a large, long room, stripped of ornamentation and painted a flat battleship gray, with most of the lighting concentrated on a raised platform at the far end. The platform held a portable organ, a weary-looking organist on a wooden chair, a polished mahogany lectern, and a male youth in a Sunday-go-to-meeting-suit of blue serge. The rest of the room was filled with many wooden chairs, many fleshy women in cheap housedresses, and a spattering of beaten men. The Greene woman was not in evidence.

A large man came hastily toward me, walking tiptoe and smiling a benign greeting. His hand sought mine and pumped my arm frantically. "Welcome, brother!" he whispered. Pressing a small hymnal into my hands, he urged me toward a section of vacant chairs. A hush seemed to descent on the congregation, and I had the uncomfortable feeling that everyone was waiting for me to be seated. I slid into a row of chairs and sat down.

The youth on the platform cleared his throat self-consciously, then raised his hands in a lazy gesture of surrender and cried: "We are all sinners!"

"Amen!" chorused those about me.

His voice gained confidence, and, for what seemed much longer than fifteen minutes, he embarked on a confused but emphatic lecture on sin. With considerable waving of arms and pounding on the lectern, he managed to go around and about this thesis several times, arousing numerous joyous amens from his audience. I stared at a blue-and-white banner over his head which proclaimed HEAVEN IS HAPPINESS and decided he was a local seminary student gathering credits in pulpit oratory, temporarily assigned to the Brotherhood as a warmer-upper for Doctor Greene. Two hymns later this theory was borne out, for, with somewhat awkward timing, the platform lights dimmed suddenly, a spotlight circled the area behind the lectern, and a slim, dark-haired figure wearing a flowing black cassock stepped through the rear doorway. She moved slowly into the beam of the spotlight and spread her arms in the classic gesture of loving welcome.

The audience rose and, without benefit of organ, launched. into *Our Troubles Will be Washed Away*. Patricia Greene stood poised before the swaying men and women, a soft smile on her lips, reminding me of a picture of Joan of Arc before the fire was lit. As I watched, her dark eyes moved toward me and seemed to linger for a moment. Then they moved, slowly, across the congregation, betraying nothing, and her arms dropped to her sides.

The song came to an end and the audience sank back on the chairs. She waited a full minute. Then, gripping the sides of the lectern with her pale hands, she began talking in a ringing, assured voice. Her subject was the duty of man and, judging by the smooth way she handled it, it was a sermon which she had delivered often or which she had stolen verbatim from a more gifted source. I stared at her, fascinated by the role she was playing, and tried to reconcile her with the naked, frightened woman who had awakened in my arms that morning.

I was so absorbed in puzzling over the contradiction that I scarcely heard her final peroration. The roar of the organ shattered my thoughts, and I saw that she was standing with her head bowed and her arms spread in pious supplication. The congregation rose and joined in an enthusiastic chorus of *Onward, Christian Soldiers*. As the chorus came to an end, a tall, spare man in black garb rose from beside the platform, ascended it slowly, and strolled front and center to meet Doctor Greene. With a start, I recognized the heavy-browed gentleman the jug troupe had robbed on the steps of the bank that morning!

111

TOO YOUNG TO DIE

As though well-cued, the woman turned, smiling graciously, as he approached, and put her hands in his. Then, a beaming duet, they faced the congregation together and lifted their arms. This apparently was a signal for the ushers, for, as the organ began wheezing *Bringing In The Sheaves,* four men sprang up and began circulating wicker collection baskets. During the distraction of pocket-reaching and purse-opening which followed, Doctor Greene turned her head slightly and murmured something to the man in black. He nodded gravely, and, while the Doctor made a stately exit through the rear door, he descended from the platform. Walking like someone buried in weighty and pious thoughts, he proceeded to the last row of chairs where, clasping his bony hands behind him, he bent to whisper something to a seated man. The man looked up, frowned, and I saw his lips move in quick question. I saw that he was a large man, no longer young, with big bones and the shoulders of a guy used to hard work. Still talking, they walked to the door through which Doctor Greene had gone. I slid out of my seat and began working my way past the rows of quarter-clutching brethren.

The door opened a moment before I reached it and the man in black emerged. His glance was quick and appraising, yet guarded, like that of an actor counting the house. "May I help you, brother?" he asked, using mostly chest tones and pushing his pock-marked face toward me.

"I'm looking for Doctor Greene." I tried to sound properly humble.

"Ah, yes." He nodded gravely, like a respectful funeral director, and stroked his high-beaked nose with a spatulate finger. "The Doctor is resting. If it has to do with the affairs of the Brotherhood, perhaps I may assist you."

"It's personal."

"I see." He frowned. "Come with me, please."

112

THE FLESH PEDDLERS

I followed him. The door opened onto a narrow, dimly lighted corridor. He led me at a leisurely pace to a second door, rapped with his knuckles, then twisted the knob and stepped back so I could precede him. As soon as I stepped past him, I realized my mistake—but it was too late. His hands rammed into my back like a charging bull, propelling me violently into the gloom of a cluttered alley.

I tripped, banged against a steel garbage drum, and fell on my side amid a pile of soggy cartons. Instictively, I flung out my arms and tried to roll.

Hands grabbed me, tore at my clothes, dragged me to my feet. I swung blindly and got a multi-colored punch in the eye for my trouble. There were three of them, I realized, all damned big and capable of doing a complete job. I had no desire to be a dead hero, so I went limp and tried to crumple to the ground. No dice. A shoe pounded my tail and the hands jerked me roughly erect, forcing me either to stumble forward down the dingy unlighted alley or to take a chance on not kissing a broken bottle with my face.

At the end of the alley another guy joined us. I recognized him vaguely as the one the man in black had spoken to.

"Everything okay?" he asked harshly.

"Yeah," the guy who was torturing my left arm muttered.

"Kick him where it hurts," someone suggested.

I winced inwardly and stumbled forward, letting them guide me to an enclosure at the end of the alley. The stink was thick enough to slice. Frankly, I was scared. If I had seen the slightest chance to make a break, I'd have taken it. But four against one is a sucker's odds, and I'd been sucker enough.

Grunting and cursing, they shoved me against an iron grill which covered the unglassed hole of a window. Then they started to slap me around. At first it didn't hurt, it just made me feel disgusted and trapped and helpless. But they

113

were vicious. They'd slam me against the grill. Instinctively, I'd try to bound away from it. Then they'd slam me against it again. Like cats tormenting a mouse.

I hadn't the slightest desire to be a hero, but there's a limit to the amount of mauling a man can take without reaction. So when I saw the hazy outline of a chin in front of me, I swung at it hard. The blow landed on his chest and with a curse, he staggered back. It was what they wanted. They started cutting at me with their open hands, Chinese fashion, each blow feeling like the edge of a heavy board pounding into me. I tried to run. One of them laughed, tripped me, and the others threw me back against the grill.

It was savage. They worked me over slowly at first, using the edges of their hands, then they switched to fists. The first blow was a short jab in my guts, just under my breastbone. The air whooshed out of me and pain shot through me like liquid fire. A blow caught me in the face. I lashed out blind and felt the sting of my knuckles against a shoulder. They laughed and started using their feet too.

Consciousness began to slip from me. Suddenly they stopped and stepped back. I groaned and fell to my knees. Immediately, hands clawed into my shoulders and hurled me back against the grill, propping me erect. I realized dimly that another person had come down the alley and was standing in front of me. I groaned again and flung an arm across my eyes. A hand slapped at my arm, knocking it down. Things began to swim back into focus, and, like a dying man who is grateful for small things, I realized with an insane sort of pleasure that the stink around me had become somewhat sweeter. Then I turned and saw her.

"Let this be a lesson to you," she said softly. The blackness of her hair and gown merged into the gloom, making her thin white face seem to float in front of me. "Next time they'll kill you."

114

My throat rattled inarticulately.

"Next time they'll kill you," she repeated. Her eyes seemed to swell and explode. "Understand?"

I passed out. When consciousness returned, the heavy stink of decaying refuse was in my nostrils. I moaned and moved my head. A can rolled lethargically away, taking a minor part of the stink with it. I tried to get to my knees. It was like arousing a swarm of pain. Gritting my teeth, I drew my legs under me and inched forward a little, suppressing the cry of anguish which tried to screech from my lips. Somehow, I got my eyes open. I was still in the alley. It was still night.

And "Doctor" Greene was gone . . .

PART II

Hymn to Hell

Ten

Honest To Mallory

I MUST HAVE PASSED out again, for the next thing I remember is hearing a warning shout and feeling the white glare of a powerful spotlight burning into my eyes.

"Another damned wino," someone growled.

"We'd better pick him up," another voice said. "Somebody's liable to run over him."

"Why not call the district?"

My stomach flopped despairingly. Cops!

"Hell, we'd have to sit around and wait for them. We can drop him off on the way in."

"Okay, okay!" Heavy feet came toward me and a hand turned me onto my back. I groaned as pain shot through my shoulder. "Hey, looks like the guy's been rolled!"

"The hell you say." A car door opened and more heavy feet approached.

"He's had a beating. See?" A flashlight flicked about me.

"Yeah. Hey, wait a minute. Flash his face again, Pete." There was a moment of silence, then a snort of astonishment. "Hell, it's Carl Good!"

"Good? We got a pick-up on him, haven't we?"

"Yeah. See if anything's broken."

A hand probed my arms and legs cautiously, then moved about my body, patting my pockets. Pain melted the numbness which had engulfed me and I managed to roll my head weakly. Instantly, a voice asked:

"You okay, Good?"

"Yeah." It was a garbled syllable and it was several seconds before I realized that it was my own voice.

"Think you can get up?"

"Try." Then, a little stronger: "Help . . . me."

"Get his other arm, Pete. Easy, now." They lifted me slowly, clasping me about the waist with strong arms, and set me on my feet. My knees buckled and I wobbled crazily. They tightened their grip and half-carried, half-pushed me to their car. With a grateful sigh, I collapsed on the seat. The hands went over me again, probing gently for wounds and broken bones.

"A slug of something might help, lieutenant."

"It might, at that. There's a saloon on the corner, Pete."

"Right."

I sighed and tried to relax, but my mind was clearing rapidly and the fact that I'd fallen into the hands of the cops was ballooning into a fear which deadened the pain in my limbs and body. Out of the frying pan into the fire. It might have been better if the punks had killed me . . .

"Take a belt of this, Good." A circle of glass pressed against my lips. "Careful, it's bonded bourbon."

I sucked, swallowed, then coughed violently as the liquor burned down my throat. It etched a flaming path to my stomach, spread blissfully, and a warm tingling suffused my insides. I sucked and swallowed again. "Thanks." I gasped. "Okay, now."

I opened my eyes. They were in plainclothes; sport shirts and rumpled slacks. The one holding a half-pint bottle was dark-haired, lean-faced, built like a swimmer. A snub-nosed belly-gun was tucked into the belt of his slacks. The other cop was older. He sat sidewise in front, looking at me over the back of the seat and, in the shadows of the small sedan, his thin face seemed Mephistophelean. He shifted restlessly as I looked at him and a corner of his mouth twitched.

"I'm Lieutenant Mallory," he said quietly. "Scotland Yard Detail. This is Sergeant Russin. We were cruising around, doing a little checking, and Pete happened to spot you. Feel better now?"

"Yeah." I struggled into a more comfortable position.

"Who beat you up?"

"Three or four guys."

"Know them?"

"No."

"How did it happen?"

"They tricked me into the alley and jumped me."

"Right here?"

"The other end of the block, I think. Behind the Brotherhood."

"The Brotherhood?" Interest quickened in his voice. "What were you doing there?"

I shrugged. "Getting religion, maybe."

Sergeant Russin laughed. "I'll bet," he said.

Mallory smiled mirthlessly. "I suppose you know there's a *Wanted* order out for you."

"Somebody mentioned it." I met his eyes. "It's a frame, lieutenant. Put that in the record."

Instead of commenting on my statement, Mallory looked at Russin and said: "We better get out of here, Pete. It's about time for a cruiser to be around."

"Okay." Russin capped the bottle he had been holding, tossed it onto the cushion beside me, and went around to the driver's seat. As he climbed behind the wheel, he asked: "Where to, lieutenant?"

Mallory thought a moment. "Take him to my place."

I lifted my eyebrows a little but said nothing. Russin got the car moving and circled toward Clark Street, then headed north. At Diversey and Clark he parked beside an apartment building and turned off the ignition.

Mallory stared up and down the street as though making certain that we were unobserved. "Think you can walk?" he asked.

"I'm okay," I said. I got out of the car gingerly, weaving with pain, and noticed that the sedan was a plain greenish Pontiac, rather elderly, instead of the black Ford usually assigned to police officers. Russin came around and offered me his arm. Ignoring it, I hobbled into the building. Mallory strode ahead and held the door.

Mallory had a small, neat kitchenette on the fifth floor which contained a sofa bed, several chairs, a rack filled with ancient pipes, and not much else. He turned on lights, removed a pearl-handled belly-gun from his belt, plopped into a Morris chair and selected a short-stemmed briar from the rack. I sank into a chair. Russin went to a sink in the corner, drank a glass of water, then dropped onto the sofa bed.

I watched Mallory tamp tobacco into his pipe. While he was holding a match to it, I said: "You're a hell of a cop."

"Think so?" He sounded amused. "Why?"

"You pick up a wanted man in an alley and you buy him a drink. You're a lieutenant of detectives, but you're driving a broken-down bus, probably on your own time." I gestured broadly at the room. "And you're living in a cigarbox instead of a joint befitting your income."

Mallory puffed on his pipe for a moment. In the lighted room, the Mephistophelean effect wasn't as pronounced as it had been in the sedan. He had strong, taut features, thin hair, shading from brown to gray and a chin which jutted a little. His body was medium in build, but he gave the impression of being wiry and high-strung.

"I've been a cop nearly twenty years," he said abruptly, "and a lieutenant for three. Know what I make?"

"Plenty," I said succinctly.

"From graft, I suppose?"

"You didn't become a cop because you wanted to wear a gun, did you?" I asked.

"Maybe I did." He blew a thin cloud of smoke at me. "My old man was a cop, got killed chasing a two-story worker down a dark alley. He didn't take graft and I didn't wear shoes regularly until I got to high school."

"But you signed up anyway."

"Sure. But not because I was in love with the uniform, and not because I expected to get my hands into other people's cash registers. God knows I haven't. You've seen the police salary schedules. The newspapers run them every time somebody talks about increasing cops' pay. A lieutenant draws a little better than five grand a year."

"Balls," I said pointedly. "You're not talking to the Citizens' Crime Committee."

"That's the truth." He took the pipe out of his mouth and stared at it as though it were defective. "I'm assigned to the Scotland Yard Detail. That means that the commissioner has confidence in me. In a way, it's a desirable spot because I'm pretty much my own boss and can dig where I think digging is necessary. But the salary is less than a lot of soda jerks make. I drive my own car. I wear my own clothes. I have to kick in to a pension fund. I buy my own bullets and guns. And, more often than not, I work around the clock. So there isn't a hell of a lot of dough in it. You see, there are all kinds of cops, Good, just like there are all kinds of people. I've tried to be an honest cop."

"You must feel damned lonely."

"Sometimes." Mallory smiled slightly. "But a lot of cops are honest, Good. Believe it or not. In the long run it pays, I think. At least, I don't have to flinch every time I face a mirror. I can shave without hoping I'll cut my throat."

"This is certainly a new approach," I commented.

"I'm trying to lay a firm basis for understanding," Mallory said. "I could strong-arm you and I could shovel crap, too. But that isn't the way I operate. I want you to know my rules of the game; once they're understood, I expect you to respect them. Just as I'll respect yours. I happen to know that you've been a square-shooter as a private eye goes, and I seem to remember that you cooperated with us on a couple of homicides a year or so ago. I think that entitles you to some consideration and, if it's in my power, I'll see that you get it."

"Thanks." I said it dryly.

"The beating you got wasn't faked. That's a point in your favor," Mallory went on, scowling faintly. "I'm not familiar with all the details of the Greene killing, but I understand Captain Stone ordered your arrest. You said it was a frame. Who do you think is framing you? Captain Stone?"

I snorted. "Stone doesn't know his tail from his thumb."

"Then what's your gripe?"

"Let me ask you a question, Mallory. Suppose I tell you the whole story. Suppose I convince you that something's rotten. Captain Stone ordered my pick-up, and he outranks you. He runs the district. What happens to me?"

"I don't take orders from Stone." Mallory's eyes glinted. "I report directly to the commissioner."

"But I've got a living to make, and a hell of a lot of my business is in Stone's district."

"You're not a complete idiot, Good—and neither am I.

This sparring isn't necessary." A hard note entered Mallory's voice. "We both know that Stone's district is full of gamblers, thieves, prostitutes, fags and weed peddlers. Also, we both know that they couldn't exist without police knowledge. The lid has been on. Part of my job is to keep it on. It's Stone's job, too, of course, but the fact that vice and gambling continue in the district is a pretty good indication that there's a payoff or a fix operating. But knowing a thing like that is one thing—and proving it is another. If you can hand me tangible proof that Stone is crooked or incompetent, he'll be out on his can in a hurry."

What he said was true enough, but it wasn't exactly inside information. The newspapers had been crying the same story for years. Still every once in a while a sincere crusader comes up through the ranks and somehow the crackle in Mallory's voice and eyes convinced me that he was sincere. Whether he'd actually go to bat for me was another matter. But I didn't have much of a choice; in fact, I didn't have any choice at all.

"Well, this isn't proof," I said, "but where there's stink there's usually something rotten. Try it for size."

I gave them the whole story.

While I talked, Lieutenant Mallory smoked quietly and drummed his fingers silently on the arm of his chair. Sergeant Russin got out a pack of cigarettes and blew smoke rings at a fading lithograph of a kneeling Indian which hung on the wall behind Mallory's head. When I finished, Mallory grunted and dropped his pipe into a chipped ceramic bowl. He eyed Russin questioningly.

"What do you think, Pete?" he asked.

"Good may have stumbled onto something," Russin said. "At least, it hangs together."

"What else?" Mallory probed.

"Stone was out of his district."

"Right." Mallory rubbed his chin. "I wondered if you'd notice that. It strikes me as damned queer."

"What do you mean?" I asked.

"You said Stone's man, Sergeant Peters, picked you up at Diversey and Pinegrove. That's not part of Stone's district," Mallory explained. "It suggests that he was stretching his authority for a purpose."

"For chrissake," I muttered, "that's right. Neither of the killings were in the Chicago Avenue area. Diversey is part of the Park District, isn't it?"

Mallory nodded. "And as a matter of routine, virtually all homicides are handled from central headquarters. Normally, the district captain reports a homicide in his area to central headquarters and a squad operating out of there takes over. It's not unusual for a captain to take an interest in killings in his own district, but Stone definitely was exceeding his authority in operating out of his command. What happened to the sheets and stuff that you took out of that Hidalgo Terrace apartment?"

"I think they were accidentally destroyed."

Mallory twitched an eyebrow. "And the packet you lifted from Greene?"

"It's on its way to General Delivery."

"What was in it?"

"Morphine. About fifteen grand worth."

Sergeant Russin whistled softly. "Pure?" he asked.

"I think so."

"That represents a lot of dough. Hasn't anybody tried to hit you for it?"

"No one has mentioned it."

Mallory looked puzzled. "That's damned odd, too," he said. "Properly cut, that much morphine is worth a fortune. Even if Greene were peddling—"

"He wasn't," I interrupted. "I checked."

126

"Who'd you check with?"

I grinned. "An unimpeachable source," I quoted.

"You probably asked Morrie Tannen to get a line on it for you," Mallory speculated shrewdly. "If that's your source, it's as good as gospel. But Greene wasn't carrying that can around for a good-luck piece. It was a business asset—and Greene's racket was flesh. He must have been finagling a trade of some sort."

"That much dope would buy a hell of a lot of flesh," I commented.

"Not high-class flesh," Mallory corrected, "and, from what I've gathered, Greene was shooting for big-fee stuff." Mallory paused, scowling, then added: "It could be that one of the smaller operators wanted to switch to dope. Sometimes girls are a headache, you know. Greene may have been working on a deal: the dope for a string of girls."

"Don't forget that Betty Brandt was a valuable property," I pointed out. "She got it at nearly the same time that Roy Greene did."

"That's right." Mallory frowned thoughtfully.

"The thing that gets me," Sergeant Russin said, "is this Brotherhood deal. The lieutenant and I have had our eyes on it for quite a while, but we were never able to hook it together. Stone must have known the set-up."

"Of course," Mallory shrugged. "It's a smart gimmick. I got interested in the Brotherhood several months ago, and I did some checking. Outwardly, at least, it's operated legitimately. I've talked to several of the members. They swear that Doctor Greene has a genuine call. Organizations like this are ticklish things to investigate. The Constitution guarantees them freedom from persecution, and city policy is to lean over backward if necessary so as not to arouse public indignation. You've been on the southside. There's a sect of some kind in every other building on many of the streets, and a lot of them are nothing more than fortune-tellers, spiritualists and voodoo charm peddlers, but we can't touch them."

"You mean she's a *bona fide* cleric?" I asked incredulously.

"She's got a sheepskin which says she's a Doctor of Divinity, also a Doctor of Philosophy, if that's what you mean," Mallory stated. "The college which issued it was an obscure jerkwater outfit in Indiana, if I remember correctly. Closed down, now. For all I know, it could have been nothing more or less than a mail-order diploma-mill. But she's got the diplomas—in a frame on the wall of her office."

"How about checking her background?" I asked.

"That's routine now that we know that there's something fishy. I'm more interested in her sources of income." His lips tightened. "If it works the way you say, that D.D. degree of hers is going to stand for dead duck."

"What about Stone?"

"Stone's not invulnerable. To begin with, I intend to worry him a little. He stuck his neck out this morning by stepping out of his territory, so maybe if I push him a little he'll get nervous and give us a chance to chop him down." A bleak look pierced his eyes. "It's bad enough when a beat cop is crooked. If Captain Stone is taking a cut from the flesh and dope rackets, he deserves to be chopped; in fact, I'd take a great deal of personal pleasure in shooting him myself."

I knew that Chicago, like every town large or small, had its share of dishonest officials, including cops. But I knew also that, by and large, the police tried to do an honest job, and honest men on the force far outnumbered the occasional bad pennies who seemed to be turning up all the time to make things rough for yours truly. Was my luck changing? Had I run across a real law-enforcer at

128

last, intelligent enough to know the score—independent enough to do his sworn duty at all costs?

It was hard to believe, yet this Mallory certainly differed a lot from, for instance, Captain Stone.

"There's too much temptation in that district."

"Maybe you're right," Mallory admitted, "but Stone is the immediate problem. As I understand it, the only loose ends still hanging are a guy named Samp Constantine, who was cannoning for Zike, and a girl named Lucy who may have worked with Betty Brandt."

"Don't forget Doctor Dick Williams," I reminded him.

"The double-sucker." Mallory nodded. "I'll see if our B of I has a record on him. It's just possible that he's an ex-con; if he is, we'll pick him up for questioning. This girl Lucy, though. What about her? . . . Did you hear her last name?"

"Tina didn't know."

"Did Tina get a look at her?"

"No. She said Betty Brandt had mentioned her, and I got the impression that it had happened in the course of casual conversation. Tina thought the two girls might have worked together."

"Too bad." Mallory stood up. "Well, I'll do what I can with what you've given me. In the meantime, I want you to park here and keep out of circulation."

"Hell, lieutenant," I protested, "I can—"

Mallory gave me a hard look. "I'm giving you a break, Good. According to the rules, I ought to run you in. Don't forget, there are 7,000 cops in Chicago and they're all looking for you. You might run into a cop with ideas different from mine." He jerked his head toward the sofa bed. "You can flop there tonight. A little rest won't hurt you." He stretched lazily, then picked up the pearl-handled gun and thrust it into the waistband of his trousers. "You'll be safe here. I'll wake you when I get back."

"When will that be?"

He shrugged. "Who knows? Sometimes I work around the clock. Come on, Pete, let's move."

They went out, closing the door quietly.

Eleven

Blonde without Buttons

I TURNED OUT THE lights and crossed to the window. Mallory and Russin came out of the building and climbed into the green Pontiac. They sat there several minutes, as though discussing ways and means of procedure, then the sedan roared to life, made a U-turn, and went east on Diversey. I watched its tail-light disappear in the vicinity of Lincoln Park, then I studied the intersection below me.

The shoe store was dark, but the corner cigar store and Walgreen's drugstore were brightly lit. It was past midnight and there were few pedestrians. In front of the Hollywood Cafe, three squad cars were parked, each with a lone cop behind the wheel listening to the radio calls. The others would be at the counter inside, I knew, drinking coffee on city time. Across the street, farther down the block, a red neon sign alternately flashed DOBKIN, then CAMERAS, at regular intervals. I stared at it a long time and, at equally regular intervals, almost as though triggered by the sign, two questions began flashing through my mind: *Is Mallory on the level?* Then: *What if he isn't?*

I left the window and turned the lights on again. The bathroom door was ajar. I pushed it open and switched on

131

the light over the medicine cabinet. A battered, haggard face, hardly recognizable as my own, peered at me from the mirror. I washed desultorily, drying myself on the single thin hand-towel which hung from a nickeled bar. A professional private cop acquires habits, and one of mine has to do with medicine cabinets. To most people, they're a catch-all for intimate items and a great deal can be learned from them. I eyed the cabinet a moment, then opened it—and blinked. It contained a razor, a used packet of ten-cent blades, a nearly dead tube of toothpaste, a fairly new toothbrush. Nothing else. I closed the cabinet door and switched off the light.

Moving automatically, I went to the sofa bed and lifted up the seat, exposing the bedding compartment. It contained a blanket old enough to have been used by George Washington and a sheet which had seen much use. A glint of light-colored material in a far corner caught my eye. I got down on my knees and strained an arm toward it. My shoulders had stiffened and the muscles in my arm screamed in protest, but I got my fingers to it. It was soft and silken and included an elastic of some sort. Sweating a little from the pain and the exertion, I got up and let the seat fall back into place. I stared at my prize. It was a cute nylon pantie, medium-sized, pink as the flesh of the girl who had undoubtedly worn it, and machine-embroidered in blue silken thread across the left-front with the curious legend: Tuesday.

I stood there a moment, the pantie and my lower jaw both dangling. After a while, like a bedroom moron, I crumpled it into a nylon ball and sniffed at it. It had a delicate powdery scent, faintly reminiscent of lavender or lilacs. A blonde scent—or an old woman's! But it wouldn't be like an old woman to wear such fancy pants. I thrust the pantie deep into a trouser pocket.

132

HYMN TO HELL

At the back of my mind, a familiar alarm bell was beginning to jangle. Moving quickly now, I went to the small refrigerator which nestled beneath a miniature kitchen sink and pulled on its chrome handle. The door opened, revealing two cans of beer and a baby roach which scuttled desperately for cover. I slammed the door shut and began opening cabinets. I found a set of dusty dishes, a few soiled glasses, a third of a fifth of Seagrams VO, and many antique crumbs. Mallory, obviously, did little cooking.

The closet contained a raincoat and a necktie. A conviction was growing in me and, almost angrily, I began jerking out the drawers of a small chest which stood near the sofa bed. Except for a few soiled shirts, the drawers were empty. I moved to the center of the room, breathing heavily, and forced my mind to admit a new fact: the apartment was a drop. Mallory didn't live here.

An instant later I had the lights off again and was peering through the window. Several pairs of loitering lovers were strolling east on Diversey but in general the street was quiet. One of the squad cars had departed. The neon sign was still flashing. Abruptly, one of the two remaining squad cars pulled away from the Hollywood Cafe, rounded the corner, and parked on the Clark Street side of Walgreen's. No one got out.

I grunted and twisted my head around to give Diversey a more thorough scrutiny. I finally found what I had vaguely suspected: west of the apartment building, partially concealed by the shadows cast by a garage on the south side of the street, another squad car was parked. Its headlights were extinguished and I might have missed it if it hadn't been for the thin gleaming antenna rod which rose from its rear fender.

I watched it closely for several minutes and caught the pinpoint glow of a cigarette. It was occupied. Like the one

133

around the corner, it was waiting.

For me?

If so, time was running out. I crossed the room and un-latched the door, listening intently before opening it. The carpeted corridor ran straight through to the rear of the building. Locking the door behind me, I ran lightly to the end of the corridor, where an open window beckoned. I climbed out of the window, clinging to a narrow fire-escape. I hesitated a moment, weighing my chances of being ob-served; necessity forced me forward, for there was no other way of reaching the ground. I crawled down two flights, half-slid down the next two, then paused to deliberate.

The final flight was suspended from the ground, held aloft by weights. I decided not to risk the screech of rusted metalwork and, with more pain than caution, I gripped the framework and swung myself over the side of the second-floor platform. I hung there a moment, enduring the ache and throb of my shoulders, then I relaxed my legs and dropped.

The ground pounded my knees into my belly. Groaning inwardly, I rolled over. I lay motionless, waiting for the sting of the fall to recede. Then, flooded with the harsh ne-cessity of escaping, I got to my feet and stumbled blindly through the heavy shadows which wreathed the areaway. I found concrete, then a gate, and emerged on an alley. I loped across it like a tomcat on his way to a new back fence and discovered that the alley was T-shaped. Feeling more as-sured, I followed the long bar of the T to a narrow street which was darker than an old maid's bedroom. Slowing my step to a casual stroll, I turned north and walked several blocks.

There was a thin sliver of doubt in my mind, but it looked as if Mallory was pulling something fancy. He and Russin had been prowling the alley behind the Brotherhood. It seemed odd that a lieutenant, especially one assigned to the Scotland Yard Detail, would be driving through neighborhood alleys at night. Also, he had shown less interest in details of the killings than he had in the suspected flesh racket. Maybe Mallory was bucking for a chance to get himself kicked upstairs into Stone's captaincy . . .

I circled around to Surf Street, avoiding the bright lights, and walked east. It was a very long block, and, by the time I had reached Lake Shore Drive, quite a few ideas had been sorted through and discarded. A question which had occurred to me several times previously, but which I had pushed aside as unimportant, began to loom larger and larger. What had happened to Samp Constantine, the cannon who had ducked into the Ottawa Arms with the jug troupe's loot?

A siren shrieked, slicing the air with shrill ecstasy. I stepped into an ink-blot of shadow and froze. A squad car rushed off Diversey and entered Lincoln Park, its red flasher circling wildly. I stepped back to the sidewalk, thinking about Samp Constantine.

He had wanted a kick. He had gone into the Ottawa Arms. He had been there when Tina had discovered Betty Brandt's body—and, until late that afternoon, he had failed to contact Zike, the leader of the troupe. For a professional thief to duck with his gang's pickings was virtual suicide. The least he'd get would be a shiv in the belly at some future date. Even sneak types knew better than that, and Samp Constantine was reputed to be a good cannon, a specialist used to working with a stall or two and a finger. Pulling a double-cross would not only make him a marked man; it would make it virtually impossible for him to pursue his chosen profession in the future. It didn't add. No matter how big the loot had been, it didn't add.

So what had happened to Samp Constantine?

135

I walked slowly to the corner of Lake Shore Drive and Diversey. The Ottawa Arms was a block away. I started toward it, drawn by a mixture of curiosity and desperation. I had reached the Commonwealth drugstore and was about to cross Pinegrove when the wail of another siren knifed toward me. I did double-time toward the nearest shadows— and nearly collided with a slight, elderly man who apparently had the same idea. I was halfway through a muttered apology before I recognized him.

"Well!" I said softly. "Red Dog Pyle!"

He had excellent control, but I felt the muscle in his thin arm twitch beneath my hand. "I beg your pardon," Pyle murmured in very gentlemanly tones. "I believe you have mistaken me for—"

"Like hell." I pressed him back into the shadows. "How long have you been scouting the Ottawa Arms?"

"I haven't the slightest idea what you're talking about." His face assumed a look of righteous, well-bred indignation and he tried to jerk his arm free. "If you don't release me immediately, I'll call the police."

I chuckled. "Fat chance. You're about as anxious to avoid the cops as I am. My name is Carl Good. I'm a private dick. Right now I'm hot because the cops think I'm involved in a couple killings. I saw the troupe pull that trick this morning, and I tailed Samp to the Ottawa Arms. I know he hasn't shown with the dough. I want to know what happened to him."

Red Dog's mobile face became ministerial. "You must be intoxicated, young man. I haven't the slightest idea what—"

"Look." I dug my fingers into his arm. "It's smart for you to play it cagey, but there isn't a hell of a lot of time left and my interests are the same as yours. Do you remember a girl named Dolly Iola? You had quite a fling with her back in the days when you were plucking daisies."

136

"Dolly?" The name aws like a shot in the arm. He stiffened apprehensively, then he ceased struggling. "Why, yes. I remember a girl named Dolly."

"There's only one Dolly. Big, beautiful, dark-haired, built like a statue. I was talking to her this afternoon. I told her that I'd seen you. She's running a joint called the Player's Club on Clark Street, but she'd like to shoot her dough into a plushier joint on Michigan Avenue, the kind of deal which requires a lot of front and a smooth operator to handle the tables. I told her you might be available. She's anxious to talk to you about it."

"Dolly Iola." His memory stroked the syllables fondly. "Wants to open a plush joint, eh?"

"She hasn't aged, either," I went on rapidly. "If anything, she has ripened. And she remembers the great time you gave her. It would be a good spot for you, a hell of a lot better than fingering for a small-time troupe. You'd be working with the kind of suckers you understand."

"Umm." He gave me an airy smile of understanding. "What's your angle?"

"I need some straight answers," I said bluntly. "There's a phone booth in the drugstore. I want you to call the Player's Club and talk to Dolly. Ask her if I'm right or wrong."

In the deep shadows, Pyle's face seemed to darken malevolently. But his voice remained even and controlled. "What's her number?"

"Look it up in the directory so you'll know it's on the level."

"Where will you be?"

"Right here."

He nodded and stepped briskly out of the shadows, into the lemon square of light cast by the drugstore's window. He walked with a spruce, springy step, looking like an elderly banker on his way to purchase a nocturnal ice cream

137

soda. I moved back into the shadows and waited. Ten minutes passed on caterpillar feet, then he returned, looking even more dapper than before. He didn't massage his hands eagerly, but his voice managed to impart that effect.

"I talked to Dolly," he said briskly. "She said you were right."

"Fine," I said. "I figure that neither you nor Zike has heard from Samp."

"True." His head jerked. "The bastard—"

"How much was the mark carrying?" I interrupted.

"A bundle. Ten grand, at least."

"Did he cash a check, or make a savings withdrawal, or what?"

"He wrote out a counter check and cashed it."

"How did you pick him?"

"Somebody tipped off Zike to watch him."

"So Zike sent you in?"

He nodded.

"I was near the counter and he looked like he might not be penny-ante. When he went to the window, I moved around where I could see the cashier dealing the dough out. The bills were big and amounted to a good bundle, so I walked on out ahead of him."

"Did you rumble him?"

"I didn't need to. He slapped the dough into a wallet and put it into his coat pocket. I saw him."

"Okay. Who picked the jug?"

"Zike. He'd been around, looking for a likely location."

"Did he mention that a loaded doctor might be spotted there?"

"Yes." Red Dog nodded his head emphatically. "I told you, he got this tip."

"Is this the first job you've pulled with them?"

"I've only been in the city a couple of days."

"Have you talked to Zike recently?"

"I called him about an hour ago."

"Had he heard from Samp?"

"No. He was screaming that everybody had double-crossed him."

"Meaning you, too?"

"Zike knows better than that. From what he said, I gathered that Tina had been giving him a hard time."

"So what made you head for the Ottawa Arms?"

"I thought Samp might have gotten sidetracked by that girl of his."

"Tina?"

"Tina wouldn't mess with a junkie. He had another kid, one he was hitting the deck with occasionally, and I figured he might have needed a kick real bad and come here for a good one. A big jolt might have knocked him out for a while and kept him from contacting Zike."

"What girl are you talking about, Pyle? Betty Brandt?"

"Hell, Betty's dead. I can read the papers."

"Who, then?" I demanded tensely.

"A blonde he met in some joint a couple days ago. He was sounding off about her last night, but he didn't mention her name. I knew she lived here because I spotted a key he'd lifted off her."

"Were you able to spot the number of the apartment?"

"Sure." Pyle sounded faintly indignant.

My throat felt dry. "What's the number?"

"Eight-fourteen."

"You're positive?"

"I'm getting kind of old, but my eyes are still sharp."

I closed my fingers around his arm. "Look Pyle, I want you to do one thing for me, then you can head for Dolly's. I have to get into the Ottawa Arms, but I don't want the desk clerk to spot me. Will you run interference for me?"

139

"Me, a stall?" His eyebrows shot up. "It'd be the first—"

"You'll be conning her," I said quickly. "On the way in, ring for the elevator so the cage will be waiting for me. Then go to the desk and give the clerk a line about something, anything that will keep her eyes off the cage for a minute. I'll duck in and then you can break away."

"I guess I owe you something for connecting me with Dolly." Pyle nodded. "Okay."

"Go on ahead. I'll be on your heels."

Red Dog Pyle squared his shoulders, crossed the street, and walked toward the green canopy. As soon as he opened the door, I glanced up and down Pinegrove, then followed his path. When I entered the lobby, an elevator door was just opening. I strode toward it, getting a glimpse of Pyle at the desk declaiming something to the clerk about a package which should have been left there for him. My stomach flopped nervously. The clerk was engrossed, however, and didn't look up. I stepped into the elevator, pushed the door shut, and jabbed 8.

The door of 814 had been poured out of the mold from which all hotel room doors are made. I rattled my knuckles against it lightly, then tried the knob. It was locked. Frustration flooded through me. I banged my knuckles against the panel again, not so lightly. This time I got a response.

From inside, a feminine voice cried angrily. "Can't you wait a minute?"

The door opened abruptly and I found myself staring at the nakedest blonde I'd ever seen.

140

Twelve

You Can't Take It With You

SHE WAS NEARLY MY OWN height, indisputably an unbleached blonde, and built with a fleshy solidness which could be called statuesque but which impressed me as animalesque. Her breasts, no longer young, peered pinkly at me, either through force of habit or because of the slack-hipped, heavy-legged way she stood. With softer lights and a patina of pancake, her face might have looked oval, youthful, even attractive but, loose-mouthed and dull-eyed and completely void of make-up as it was, it had the appeal of an underdone griddle cake in which a capricious cook had punched holes to simulate a human mask.

"Hello, lover," she said with an air of pleased surprise. "Come on in."

Leaving the door and my mouth hanging open, she executed a wobbly about-face and did something hippy which carried her ahead of me into the apartment. I closed my mouth, then the door, and followed her into a room which looked as though it had recently been visited by a hurricane.

"Things are kind of upset,' 'she said, gesturing casually in a wide circle which nearly upset her balance. "You don't mind, do you?"

"I'm kind of upset myself," I told her.

"Sure, ain't we all?" She laughed hoarsely somewhere deep below her breasts, sending them into a brief bounce; then, bending toward the couch, she swept a pile of torn envelopes to the floor and slapped vigorously at the vacated cushion. "Here, lover, take a load off your feet."

"Thanks." I sat down gingerly.

Straightening, she stared at me for a long moment, as though trying to get me in focus, then she rubbed a forearm across her lips and muttered: "You caught me right when I was getting ready to get into the tub. Have a smoke until I finish, huh?"

"Sure."

She turned and walked unsteadily toward an inner doorway. The door closed and, an instant later, I heard a large splash, followed by a thump, like a body slipping and sitting down unexpectedly in a well-filled tub of water. "Damn!" came through the door in muted tones.

I grinned, reached for a handful of the torn envelopes, and shuffled rapidly through them. All bore the address of Miss Lucy Lamaachia in care of the Ottawa Arms. Most were of recent date and many, I noticed, had been addressed in a strong masculine hand which exhibited a penchant for deep vertical strokes.

While the sounds of vigorous bathing continued, I did a quick snoop of the room. It contained a small truckload of feminine knickknacks and dust-catchers, most of which were thrown carelessly into overflowing heaps beside radiators or under chairs. There were a lot of dresses and lingerie, some of obviously fine quality, piled on chairs and tables. The closet hangers were half-empty and the floor was piled knee-high with discarded suits, coats, and miscellaneous winter clothing. On a shelf, beside a set of pigskin luggage, I found three paper canisters, each bearing the crimson plea

142

in block letters: *DONATE TO THE BROTHERHOOD FOR SERVICE.* They were duplicates of the one I'd spotted in Betty Brandt's apartment. I shook them. Empty.

I swung the closet door shut and turned, eyeing a pile of pastel-colored dainty garments which seemed about to topple from an end-table. Whistling tonelessly, I flipped through them until I reached an assortment of panties. Near the bottom of the heap, I came across a white pantie embroidered *Sunday.* The rest of the set were below it: peach for *Monday,* pale green for *Thursday,* light blue for *Wednesday,* and a sunny beige for *Friday. Tuesday* and *Saturday* were missing. I took the crumpled pantie out of my pocket and compared it for size. It matched, accounting for *Tuesday.* Maybe girls weren't supposed to wear panties on Saturday . . .

The bathroom door opened, discharging a billow of lavender fragrance and a damp-haired blonde in a black bra and pantie set. Apparently the bath had had a tonic effect, for her eyes were brighter and she seemed better coordinated. With scarcely any wobble at all, she crossed the room, snatched a filmy black slip from a pile on a chair, and began to struggle into it, giving me an eyeful of twisting torso and a glimpse of the word *Saturday* on the edge of her pantie. I might have known.

As though I weren't there, she strode about the room, accumulating items here and there and donning them as she went. A garter belt followed the slip, then nylons, a blouse of transparent net, high-heeled ankle-strap slippers, and, finally, a shiny black skirt of many pleats and much material. The clothes improved her; in fact, when she stepped into the skirt, my corpuscles rustled a little and it wasn't from prickly heat.

She stopped with the zipper halfway up and stared as

143

though seeing me for the first time. "Say, who the hell are you?" she asked throatily.

An odd noise, which I had intended as a mocking laugh, came out of my throat. "You mean you don't remember?" I asked.

Her mouth tightened. "Who let you in?"

"You did."

"No kidding." She said it matter-of-factly, as though the information wasn't exactly startling. "You must have come in right after I took a jolt. Who are you, anyway?"

"Friend of a friend."

"That routine, huh?" She zippered the skirt and slapped it down evenly around her legs. "Well, you're too late. You can beat it."

"Look, Lucy, I just want—"

"Sure, sure, you just want what all the guys want!" Acid dripped from the words. "Well, you can tell them that Lucy has other ideas. They'll give you somebody else's number."

"But I'm interested in you."

"The think you're interested in, all the girls got."

"Not like you."

"Take your flattery and stick it."

"It isn't flattery. According to my friend, you're the only one who's got it."

"Huh!" She emitted an unladylike snort, twisting her legs one by one so she could bend back and inspect the seams. "Say, who is this friend of yours? Hasn't he got a name?"

I let silence grow between us until she had both seams straightened satisfactorily, then I said: "Sure, he's got a name. Mallory!"

Her head swung around and she showed me the kind of a face every man dreams about at least once—in a nightmare. Her jaw hung loosely for a moment, expressing min-

144

gled surprise and terror, and her eyes stared with the abject
lifelessness of blown lamp bulbs. She managed to ask
hoarsely. "W-who?"

I smiled thinly. "Lieutenant Mallory. Don't tell me you've
forgotten him."

"That louse." A muscle in her throat was doing a nervous
pizzicato. "What's he want?"

"He wants the dough."

"Dough? Are you nuts?" Her voice rose an octave. "What
dough?"

"The dough you got from Samp."

"I didn't get any dough from Samp!" Womanlike, she
looked me right in the eye and enunciated the lie with more
violence than she would have given the truth.

"Mallory thinks you did."

She spat a suggestion which, if he had been capable of it,
would have gotten Mallory top billing as a stag act. "And
that goes for you, too!" she added.

"Samp was here this morning. Who got the dough if you
didn't?"

"How would I know?" She came toward me, breasts heaving and arms outstretched in an obvious preliminary to the
woman-against-man maneuver she had probably been using
with success since her fifth birthday. "Samp, the stupid
jerk, came here and said he needed a kick. I gave him a
small one, right out of the goodness of my heart—and honest
to God, that's all I did. He didn't mention any money." She
sank beside me, hands kneading my arm.

"You knew he'd pulled a job."

"I didn't! He came in here carrying the monkey on his
back and I gave him a small kick, just enough to keep him
going. Mallory can't make anything of that!"

"Samp was carrying ten grand."

"Why, the cheap, chiseling jerk!" Her mouth flapped in-

145

dignantly. "He didn't even offer to pay for the stuff he used!"

"Turn it off, Lucy." I pried her fingers from my arm. "Girls like you don't toss things around unless you can collect, and Samp was broke most of the time. You knew Samp stood to make a score. He probably bragged to you about it last night. When he ran in here this morning, you knew he had clicked and you saw a chance to get your hands on some big money. You can't buy junk for peanuts, and you've been needing more and more of the stuff to keep your veins from jumping. Chasing the monkey has been taking all your dough lately; you've been having a hell of a time keeping up appearances."

"You're so smart!"

"Not really. But I'm not stupid, either. I know you've been knocking down top fees working for the Brotherhood, but I also know you've been trying to chisel extra dough by doing tricks for Mallory. If the dope wasn't keeping you drained, you'd never stoop that low. But all of a sudden you're real independent. You thought I was a customer, but you tried to give me a bum's rush." I waved a hand, indicating the mess in the room. "And you're sorting things out, getting ready to pack, leaving all your winter stuff behind. It's a dead giveaway. You've got dough, sudden dough, and you're getting ready to flutter your wings. With Samp's cash, you intend to find yourself a nice safe nest in South America."

"You've got it wrong." The edge in her voice had dulled a little. "I got some dough, sure, but I didn't have to roll a guy like Samp to get it. I had it coming for a long time and I finally collected. How I earned it is none of your damned business, but I didn't get it from Samp."

"Then what happened to him?"

"I don't know." She pushed a straggling lock of hair away from her face and stared at her lap, where her fingers

146

were trying to weave themselves into a basket. "Samp came here, like I said. I gave him a kick. I took one myself, too, and then we lay down . . . and I sort of blacked out. I don't know what happened to him. He was gone when I came out of it."

"What happened to the dough?"

"I didn't even see it. He had it, I know, but it really wasn't his and I didn't try to pry it loose, either. You may not believe this, but I kind of liked Samp. He always treated me like I was a sister, maybe, and . . . Well, he was never on the make, like most guys are! He used to drop in once in a while, and I'd give him a kick, and that's all it ever amounted to. I could relax with him, see?"

She sounded sincere and oddly enough it made a perverted sort of sense. "Did he mention his plans?" I asked.

"He was supposed to meet the others, get his share, then come back here and we were going to have a good one."

"Did he come back?"

"No." She swallowed slowly, still staring into her lap. "I . . . I slept most of the afternoon, then I got something to eat, and . . . and then I started cleaning out this mess. I thought he'd ditched me. I'd just taken a good jolt for myself and was beginning to sail real good, when I heard somebody pounding on the door, and I figured it was Samp. But it was you."

"What the hell could have happened to him?"

"Maybe he got picked up."

I shook my head. "I don't think so. Look, Lucy, is this on the level?"

"Honest to God." She crossed herself gravely.

"Who do you think killed Betty?"

"Betty?" Her jaw unhinged. "Betty Brandt?"

I nodded.

"You mean she got knocked off?"

147

"About the time Samp was here. Didn't you know?"

"No." She gulped. "Oh, my God."

"Who'd want to kill her?"

"I don't know." She sprang to her feet, glanced frantically about the room. "Christ, poor Betty. I've got to get out of here!"

I watched her closely. "Roy Greene got it too, Lucy."

"He did?" The information arrested her quick movements for a second, but apparently news of his death was no great shock. "Jesus, things are really starting to pop, aren't they?"

"Who'll get it next, Lucy? Any ideas?"

"It's not my worry." She flung open the closet and with a little leap snagged one of the suitcases on the shelf. "Little Lucy knows what's good for her, and she's on her way, but fast."

She dropped the suitcase in the center of the room, opened it, and began tossing oddments into it helter-skelter. The exertion brought a flush to her cheeks, making her look more youthful and desirable. Once again, my corpuscles rustled faintly.

"Lucy—"

She glanced up. "Instead of sitting there on your can, you could give me a hand, you know."

"You're wasting your time."

"Maybe you're wasting yours, mister."

"Something big is going on. Betty got killed for a reason."

She slapped the suitcases shut, leaned her weight on it, snapped the brass catches into position. "Jesus, I should have left this afternoon."

"Why did Betty get killed, Lucy?"

She straightened fast, as though I'd slapped her rounded rear. "Say, what is this?" She eyed me dubiously, like a child studying a bug. "I thought you said you were in with Mallory."

"Mallory doesn't talk much. I'd like to know what's going on."

"Well, if he didn't tell you, it's because it's none of your damned business." She ran to the closet, dragged down another suitcase. "Beat it or I'll call him and tell him that you're getting nosy."

I sat there a while, watching her struggle with the packing, but it was obvious that all ten points of her I.Q. were involved with plans which didn't include me. I felt certain that her story, such as it was, had been straight. Samp had been there—and had gone, taking the loot with him. I had reached another dead end.

I got to my feet. "Good luck, Lucy. I'm going."

"Be seeing you." She dropped the phrase automatically, without glancing up. When I closed the door, she was bouncing on the lid of the second suitcase.

The red EXIT light over the fire stairs caught my eye. I pushed the door open, listened a moment, then started down the concrete spiral of steps. It was very late and the low-wattage bulbs at each landing seemed conscious of the fact; their yellowish glow seemed weaker and wearier than usual. When I reached the landing of the fifth floor, I paused, remembering Tina Rogers and the unwitting strip-tease she had executed for me earlier. It was a pleasant thought and her apartment was only a few steps away. Then I recalled the angry way she had flung herself out of the taxi. With a sigh, I decided there was no use courting more trouble. Besides, business had to come before pleasure. I continued down the stairs, listening to the hollow echoes of my footsteps.

An idea insinuated itself between the stagnant layers of my mind, and I came to an abrupt halt on the second-floor landing. No one had seen Samp leave the building. What if he was still in it?

Ignoring the resounding echoes, I clattered hurriedly down the stairs.

I suddenly knew where Samp was!

Thirteen

"She's A Beast!"

THE BASEMENTS OF THE OTTAWA ARMS and the Hidalgo
Terrace, I discovered, were joined by an underground pas-
sageway and serviced by a single set of boilers located in
the basement of the larger building. Like most apartment
hotels, each of the buildings devoted a section of its basement to wire-partitioned storage lockers, designed for the
convenience of guests with trunks, bicycles, baby carriages
and odds and ends of furniture which had seen better days.
All the lockers were padlocked, I found. Except one. It was
a narrow, dusty cubicle, away from the dim light which
seeped from a ceiling fixture, and its gatelike door was fas-
tened with several strands of crudely twisted baling wire.

With my heart pounding a little, I moved away from the
door and looked back, studying the cement floor under the
oblique rays of the feeble light. A faint path was discernible in the dust, indicating that other feet had sought
the locker recently. I went back to the door, located the
ends of the wire strands, and untwisted them. With a squeaky
protest, like a young girl resisting a new swain's kiss, the
door swing toward me.

TOO YOUNG TO DIE

He wasn't a pretty sight. His body, too long for the contained to which Destiny had consigned it, had been jammed into the shallow space with the arms and legs bent together like the limbs of a praying mantis. The brown suit was no longer natty. The jacket, half torn from his shoulders, was crammed into a corner. In the feeble light which angled through the slatted door, his eyes seemed to be pushing out of his face. But there was no doubt about his identity. Samp had hit his last mark.

I stood there, staring at him with my stomach feeling like a drained bathtub. Then I forced my hands into action. There was nothing in his pockets, no blood, no evidence of a wound. I tried to press the lids down over the bulging eyeballs. They moved reluctantly, as though knowing that it was wasted effort, and, when released, they slid slowly open again. Shuddering, I let the locker door fall back into place and headed for the stairs.

The fifth floor corridor was as quiet and as deserted as a church on Monday morning. The door of 514, Betty Brandt's apartment, bore a police seal. I walked on, past the elevator doors, and approached 535. I stood in front of the door for several minutes, listening, then walked to the end of the corridor and returned. The sobbing behind the door of 535 continued. I listened to it, torn between conscience and common sense, while my heart tensed like an acrobat getting ready to leap. I lifted a hand, finally, and knuckled the door lightly.

As though cut off by a sharp scissors, the sobbing ceased.

I rapped again.

"W-who is it?" Dulcet, expectant tones, the tones of a girl wiping her nose and eyes, came closer to the door.

"Carl."

A chain rattled violently, and then a sobbing, sweetly-

152

scented girl was quivering in my arms. "Y-you c-could have
c-called me!" she accused, blinking tear-stained lashes at
me. "I-I've been phoning and p-phoning and n-nobody knew
w-where you w-were!"

"Well, gosh—" The unexpected reception had sent my re-
flexes into a spin, but I snapped out of it to the extent of
putting an arm around her and stroking her hair pacifying-
ly. "—I'm sorry, Tina. Where'd you call?"

"Y-your office, of course!"

"Hell, I haven't been there since this morning."

"A m-man answered." She dabbed at her eyes and wriggled a little, trying to close the gaping front of her red
satin wrapper; the attempt was largely unsuccessful. "I
g-guess I'm a s-sight."

"Sure, you're a mess." I grinned at her and kissed the tip
of her nose. "Turn off the waterworks and tell what the
man said."

"He j-just tried to find out w-who I was."

"They've probably got a cop staked out there. You didn't
give him your name, did you?"

"I'm not t-that dumb!"

"There's nothing to worry about, then. Why were you
calling me?"

"I wanted to t-tell you that . . . that I'd t-talked . . . to
that Doctor Greene."

"You mean you went to see her?" I suppressed the urge
to kiss her nose again; I kissed her lips instead. They were
soft and warm and a little salty, and they clung to mine for
a long time. When she pulled away from me, my heart was
jumping like wild birds. "I thought you were sore at me,"
I murmured.

"I was."

"But you aren't any more?"

"Well . . . a little."

"Why?"

"You could have called me."

"I've been busier than hell."

She laid her face against my shirt; I felt her shiver. "I guess you're right, Carl. I'm . . . I'm just upset."

"You say you went to see Doctor Greene?"

"Uh-huh."

"Learn anything?"

"She's a beast!" Tina's nails dug into my back. "I never knew that anyone could be so cold-blooded!"

"Tell me about it."

"I looked up the address of the Brotherhood in the phone book, and I went to see her. It's an old store, sort of, with a lot of chairs and a platform and—"

"I know what it looks like."

"Well, I went in and walked around and finally a man came in and asked me what I wanted. I told him I wanted to talk to Doctor Greene. He stared at me as though . . . as though I were naked, or something, and then he went upstairs and told her about me. I almost quit and ran, but I kept thinking about Betty and . . . and you, and I waited until he came back and took me upstairs."

"Wait a minute, Tina. Remember the mark Samp hit this morning, the guy who looked like an undertaker?"

"Sure."

"Did you see him there?"

"No, there was just this big man with sharp little eyes and twisted lips. She called him Tommy."

"Okay. Go on."

"She was upstairs in a sort of office, and, when this Tommy brought me in, she had a big book in front of her and she was writing notes from it onto a pad. At first, she was real pleasant and friendly, just as though I were there on a social call. But as soon as I told her I wanted a job, she

. . . she changed completely. I can't explain it, but she got hard and cold and . . . beastly."

"I can imagine."

"She wanted to know how I'd heard of her and what experience I'd had and whether I had any specialties. That's what she called it. At first, I didn't know what she was talking about. I told her a girl named Betty had mentioned her and that . . . that I'd been free-lancing. Then she explained what she meant by specialties and . . . and I guess she saw that I was shocked, because she said that, since I was so young and inexperienced, she'd have to be careful how she handled me, and I might be a lot of trouble to her, and lots of things like that. Finally, she said she needed a girl and would get me started right away, but I'd have to pose for some pictures and . . . and give her a bond."

"A bond?" I ejaculated. "What kind of a bond?"

"She said she'd spent a lot of time and money getting girls started, and some of them, as soon as they were established, tried to run off to other cities or went to work for other people, and she'd decided not to put up with it any more. She said I'd have to sign a confession saying I'd done some crime but that nobody would see it except her. But if I tried to trick her, she said she'd give it to the police and the police would cooperate with her in punishing me."

"I hope you told her where to stuff it."

"How could I? She'd have known that I was spying."

"Tina." My throat felt as tight as a rusted bolt. "You didn't sign anything, Tina, did you?"

"I had to!"

"You little fool!" I exploded. "Don't you realize that—"

"But, Carl, I'd told her I was broke and needed a job, and I'd agreed to do everything she told me. She'd promised to coach me and to buy me several hundred dollars' worth of dresses so I'd be able to go to nice places with rich clients

155

and earn bigger fees. If I'd backed out then, she'd have gotten suspicious because, the way she put it, it sounded as if I was just giving her some security for the money she was going to advance me."

"You crazy idiot! A thing like that is a loaded gun pointed at your head!"

"But I *had* to, Carl! You wanted me to find out things for you, didn't you?"

"I didn't want you to stick your neck in a noose, for God's sake! I thought you'd use your head for something besides keeping your ears apart!"

"But can't you understand?" she wailed. "I had to sign it so she wouldn't get suspicious. And since I *didn't* do anything worth writing a confession about, and since they can't prove anything, anyway, I thought it would be all right."

I groaned and strode across the room. For a moment, helpless anger clogged my throat. "Tina, honey," I croaked. "Listen to me. You did the stupidest, most idiotic thing I can imagine. You don't know how the law operates. I do. The jails are full of men who were tricked into signing confessions. With the police tie-up which the Brotherhood must have, they can railroad you into a cell so fast your teeth won't have time to click. What did you confess to, for God's sake?"

"Having a . . . a gun." Her voice was meek and chastened.

"Having a gun!" I echoed sarcastically. "It's no crime to have a gun."

"She said it was."

"Take my word for it, it isn't. Anybody can own a gun, providing they're adult and don't shoot it at people."

"It said something, I guess, about my shooting somebody."

156

"You guess!" I repeated bitterly. "For chrissake, tell me all of it. Who'd you shoot?"

"I don't know. She typed it out while I was sitting there, and I signed it, but I was too nervous to read everything that it said. I think it was a man, though. Somebody named Willens or Williams or—"

"Richard Williams?" I demanded.

"Yes, that's it, I remember now. I didn't know him, so the name didn't mean anything. They can't prove I shot at him if I don't even know him, can they?"

"You know him, Tina." I sighed and dropped into a chair. "They can prove that you know him."

"But I don't know him. The only Williams I've ever known was a boy in my high school class named Merrill Williams. I haven't seen him for years. For all I know, he's—"

"Tina," I said dully. "The mark your troupe hit this morning is named Williams. Richard Williams. They can prove that you know him. Did you happen to notice when this little episode is supposed to have taken place?"

"No." Tina frowned. "I don't think she put a date on it; at least, I didn't notice one."

"Great, just great." I felt like a man who had crawled twenty miles on his belly only to find out he had been headed in the wrong direction. "What time is it, Tina?"

She glanced at her watch. "One twenty-five."

"Where's your phone?"

"In the bedroom." She pointed at a doorway. "Carl, do you think—?" she began hesitantly.

"I don't know," I said wearily. "I simply don't know." I dragged my feet into the bedroom, sat on the edge of her bed and began dialing Morrie Tannen's number. The phone rang a long time and I sat there, listening to the metallic buzz-buzzes, until finally the line clicked and a sleepy voice growled a hello. I recognized Mrs. Tannen's voice. I asked her to wake Morrie up. After another long interval, Morrie's voice came over the wire.

"Hello, Carl. Trouble?" he asked briefly.

"Yes and no. Did you check the fix?"

"I made several inquiries. It appears to be a direct deal with Stone."

"But it's out of his district."

"That's true, but the main operation is in his district. Understand?"

I thought a moment. "Could he be splitting?"

"I doubt it." There was a shrug in Morrie's voice. "It's reciprocity, if anything."

"Okay, thanks, Morrie. Hear anything else?"

"Just what's on the radio. You're still hot and as soon as you're arrested, you're to be indicted by the grand jury. That's straight from the office of the state's attorney." A tinge of concern entered his voice. "Are you making any progress?"

"I think so. It might help if somebody tipped the cops that there's a body in the basement of the Ottawa Arms. It's in one of the storage lockers. Kid named Samp Constantine." Behind me, Tina sucked in her breath sharply. I put my hand over the mouthpiece and turned my head. She looked as though she'd just seen a walking ghost. "Sorry, kid," I said, "I forgot to mention it. Better get dressed. Hurry."

"Anything else?" Morrie asked.

"Know anybody with a line into the commissioner's office?"

The wire hummed a moment. I visualized him, crouched over the phone in his pajamas, staring at the instrument through his thick-lensed glasses. "I might," he decided.

"Tell him hell is going to start popping. Blue hell. I'm going to prove that the department is full of crooked, double-dealing cops. Find out if he's interested."

"Where can I reach you?"

"I'll call you back in an hour."

"I'm tired, Carl. Make it thirty minutes."

"All right."

I dropped the receiver onto its cradle and stood up. Tina was zippering a gray skirt and tucking in the waist of a black nylon blouse which had the opacity of cellophane. She showed me a pale, frightened face. "Where are we going?" she asked nervously.

"Out of here," I said brusquely. "The building will be full of cops in a few minutes."

"Because of—" She choked on the name. "—of Samp?"

"Yeah."

"He wasn't such a bad guy. Did they . . . did they knife him?"

I shook my head. "He was throttled. Like Betty."

"Oh." She looked sick.

"Come on, hurry up—unless you want to stay here." I started for the door. She snatched up a small black purse and ran after me. I held the elevator door for her. She got in, smiling to keep her lips from trembling, and clung to my arm. As the cage slowly descended, I put my arms around her and pulled her against me. She lifted her lips. During the kiss she trembled. I released her gently when the cage stopped. She smiled bravely and straightened her blouse.

We crossed the lobby together.

159

Fourteen

New Management

I BUNDLED TINA into a taxi and climbed in after her.

"North Park Hotel," I told the driver. He nodded and started with a lurch which flung us back against the seat. During the rattling ride south, Tina sat in a huddle beside me. I put an arm around her and drew her against me. She came willingly enough, brushing my cheek with her faintly scented hair, but there was a stiffness within her, as though she had unconsciously tightened all her inner screws and bolts in anticipation of the trouble which she felt was coming.

I paid the driver at the Clark Street entrance of the North Park Hotel and led Tina around the building to Wells Street. The street was heavily shadowed. As we left the lights of the corner taproom, Tina slid her arm through mine and gripped it tightly. I felt a tremor pass through her as our hips touched.

"Where are you going?" she asked in a husky whisper.

"The Brotherhood," I said shortly. "I've got to get that paper you signed."

"But—"

"Shhh." I squeezed her arm warningly.

HYMN TO HELL

From across the street, the building occupied by the Brotherhood looked like a long dark cigar box, the kind that holds a hundred perfectos. Beside it, on one side, darker and squatter, was an inverted strawberry box of a house, and, on the other side, an even squatter building which housed the equipment of a shoemaker. No lights were visible in the Brotherhood; in fact, the entire street was dark.

"Stay here," I told her. "If anyone comes, make yourself scarce. I'll only be a minute."

"Hurry, will you?" Her face peered at me whitely from the shadows.

"Sure." I kissed her fleetingly and crossed the street.

Somewhere in the neighborhood a dog howled; the howl ended with a series of yaps and the slam of a screen door. I gained the doorway of the building and, making as little noise as possible, tried the door. I didn't expect to find it unlocked—and it wasn't. I explored the lock with my fingers. It was old-fashioned but it held the door firmly. Breaking it would take time and make noise. I walked to the side of the building and followed a narrow sidewalk which hugged the shoemaker's domain.

The sidewalk took me straight back to the alley. I stood nonplussed for a minute or two, remembering the beating I'd received there earlier, and anger tightened my hands into fists. I edged cautiously toward the rear door. It was locked, of course; probably bolted from within. I crossed the alley and stared back at the building's silhouette. Gradually windows became discernible. They were obviously out of reach and the wall beneath them was too sheer for scaling. I studied the adjoining buildings, then searched for telephone poles. Hope was beginning to die when I noticed that one of the windows was open. I moved from side to side, making certain that what I saw wasn't merely a deceptive shadow. It wasn't. The window was open at least four inches. If I were twelve feet tall, I could reach it easily. I swore softly.

Groping for the side of the building, I located the narrow sidewalk and ran back to the street. I whistled softly. Tina stepped out of a clump of black shadows and looked toward me. I gestured urgently. She looked up and down the street, then ran toward me.

"What's the matter?" she gasped.

"I need some help." I took her hand and drew her between the buildings. She stumbled once and nearly fell, but I caught her and half-held, half-led her until we reached the alley. "Be careful," I warned, "there are a lot of bottles and cans around." I guided her past the clutter of packing cases which fringed the door, then pushed her into the heavy shadows alongside the building. "Wait here," I whispered.

I moved away, searching for a garbage can. The only one I could find was half full of decaying food which reeked worse than a six-day corpse. Gagging, I felt around on the ground and located a battered lid. I fitted it onto the can as well as I could, then I wrapped my arms around the bulky can and carried it into position beneath the open window. It rattled and screeched when I climbed onto it, but it supported my weight. I listened a moment, then raised my arms. The sill of the window was still three feet beyond my reach.

"Tina!" I called softly.

"Yes?"

I reached a hand down. "Kick off your shoes, honey."

She got the idea. I heard the scuffle of her shoes falling on the ground, then her hand was in mine. I braced myself and pulled her up beside me. She laughed softly. "Isn't there an easier way of doing this?" she whispered.

162

"I can't think of any," I admitted. "The window is part way open. I'll lift you. Push it up and climb in, then go downstairs and open the back door for me. Understand?"

"Kiss me, Carl." She swayed against me, balancing precariously.

I kissed her, then I braced myself again and made a stirrup of my hands. Her fingers dug into my shoulders, and her foot, feeling small and warm, wriggled into the stirrup and nestled firmly. Beneath me, the can wobbled erratically. I waited until the can steadied, then I whispered: "Okay, now!"

Her breasts brushed my face as she rose, then her skirt swirled above my head and I heard her hands scrape against the rough boards of the building. I strained my shoulders back, lifting her slowly and steadily. Above me, the window creaked. Then, suddenly, her foot left my hands and her knees bumped hollowly against the building. I leaped to the ground and looked up. Her legs thrashed once and her derriere did a saucy can-can movement, then she disappeared. I waited a moment, listening for sounds of alarm, then I picked up her shoes and moved toward the door. A few minutes later the bolt shot back. I slipped through the dark doorway into her arms.

"Call me Two-story Tina," she giggled nervously, a moment later. "Gosh, I never want to do that again!"

I released her and rebolted the door. The darkness inside the building was almost as complete as the silence. With difficulty, I groped my way down the corridor which led to the meeting hall. It was a dark cave full of black shadows.

"This way!" Tina whispered.

Reassured, I turned and followed her to a stairway. Her skirt swished intimately against her legs as, like a child

163

who has discovered a new game, she ran ahead. I ascended more slowly, mapping our retreat and trying to absorb the feel of the place. In my time I had prowled through plenty of queer stores and offices, but this was different; it was like treading through a musty cavern, a cavern void of the usual human smells and small sounds. I could think of no special reason for alarm but somehow the place was disquieting. Tina was waiting for me on the landing.

Her hand touched my arm. "The office is right here."

"Fine."

I stood stiffly, nerves on edge, listening intently, warned by a sixth sense. Far away, a latch clicked. A current of air licked at us briefly, then the front door slammed. Tina pressed against me, clutching my arm frantically. A chair scraped the floor and footsteps crossed the room beneath us. It was too late for retreat.

"We're trapped," I whispered. "Duck in somewhere." I pushed her toward the front of the building. Her fingers squeezed mine, then she fled silently.

The footsteps proceeded to the stairway and began to ascend, making no attempt at quietness. I spotted a faint orange glow, betraying the approach of a small flashlight's beam, and I edged into the office. Tina's slippers were still in my hand. I clutched one of them tightly, balancing it in my fist, and flattened myself behind the door. The orange glow came closer, then darted about the small room like an inquisitive tongue of flame, illuminating a cluttered flat-top desk, several well-filled bookshelves, a wooden filing cabinet, and a leather-padded chair. I stopped breathing. The beam flicked over the desk, then disappeared, cut by a figure which paced deliberately into the room. Silhouetted in the small torch's glow, I made out a man, rather tall and slender.

164

He strode directly to the desk, sat down. The flashlight rolled on the desk, aimed at nothing, and the orange glow reflected dimly from the wall behind. A gaunt hand reached for the phone. As the dial began to click I slowly took a deep breath. I wasn't certain, but something about him reminded me of the man in black.

"They found the kid," he said suddenly, without preamble. There was a pettish bite to the voice, like that of an invalid used to being pampered. "I can't help it. . . . I thought you might know. . . . She's supposed to be on her way south. . . . I don't know. I caught a report on the radio. . . . Of course . . . The sooner, the better. . . . I've got it with me, but what if. . . . . No. . . . No. . . . I don't mind saying that I don't like it. You should have let the boys finish him. . . . We ought to be realistic. . . . Certainly. . . . Don't forget, it'll cost me as much as it does you. . . . All right. . . . Yes, as planned. . . . I know her. She'll raise hell, but she'll do as she's told. . . . I'm at the hall, now. . . . Yes. . . . Use the rear door, as usual." He hung up.

I stared at the back of his head and shifted the shoe in my hand.

He dialed a second number. "Miss Lamaachia's apartment," he murmured. A long silence endured, punctuated by muted buzz-buzzes, then he said: "All right, thank you."

He lowered the receiver and sat motionless for several minutes, apparently engrossed in thought, then the hand plucked at the dial again. "I'm at the hall," he said "You'd better come immediately. . . . Yes, it's urgent. . . . I can't explain. . . . I tell you, it's urgent. . . . All right." He dropped the receiver and pushed back the chair. The flashlight's beam jerked, then moved toward the doorway. I held my breath again. Rising, he strode into the corridor, the sound of his footsteps turning toward the stairway. The stairway echoed as he descended to the first floor, then I

165

could hear him walking to the rear.

I eyed the phone, wondering if I dared try to get a call through to Morrie. I decided to chance it. I was tiptoeing toward it when a sibilant hiss from the doorway sent me spinning around. Tina, wide-eyed and scared-looking, was peering around the jamb and motioning frantically.

"Get back!" I made shooing motions. "Hurry!"

She stared at me white-faced, then obeyed. Already, the footsteps were returning. I glared at the phone helplessly, then darted toward a curtained alcove on the other side of the room. The hallway light snapped on, casting a yellow plank into the office. I pressed back against some shelves and straightened the curtain. He came up the stairway rapidly, breathing audibly, as though from sudden excitement, and turned the overhead light on. The chair creaked as he sat down. I turned my head carefully, searching for a weapon, but the alcove shelves carried only circulars, printed tracts, envelopes, and odds and ends of stationery. I glanced down at my hands, where Tina's shoes dangled. They were light, flexible, and had good heels. I smiled grimly.

Papers rustled and the chair creaked restlessly. Silence and the unmeasured passage of time filled my consciousness, reminding me that it was very early morning and that my body craved rest. The air in the room was stuffy. My eyes began to slide shut and I felt myself swaying. Then a door slammed.

The short, rapid, tappity-tap of feminine footsteps crossed the floor downstairs and, like a warning maraca-beat, came up the stairs. A woman's voice, tight with suppressed fury, said: "What are you doing in my office, Dick?"

The chair creaked faintly. "Waiting for you, Doctor. It took you long enough to get here."

"Get away from my desk!"

"In a moment." Papers rustled. "I have a matter of grave importance to discuss with you, Doctor."

"It had better be important! You got me out of bed."

"A member of the Brotherhood brought this to me."

The paper rustled again. "Doctor" Greene sucked in her breath. "So this is your wicked game," she said quietly. "I wondered if some moron had gone to the trouble of taking a picture. I never thought it would be you, Dick."

"You don't deny it's true?" His voice sounded sepulchral.

"It's a photograph, isn't it?" Her shoes rasped against the floor, as though she had shifted her balance.

"You confess that you have been guilty of lewd and lascivious behavior with a man not your husband?"

"I confess nothing, particularly to you, Dick." She moved closer to him. "What do you think you're up to, anyway?"

"I'm interested in the good name of the Brotherhood, Doctor."

"Oh, crap!" She spat an obscenity. "You're not addressing an idiot, Dick. Say what you mean. I had an idea that you were getting a little too big for your collar, but I didn't think you'd be this crude. What do you want?"

There was a freighted silence for a minute, then, apparently abandoning the ecclesiastical masquerade, the man said: "This is a showdown, Pat. I want you out."

"Why?"

"I don't like your management."

"So you don't like my management!" There was a smile in her voice, a dry-iced smile. "Three years ago you crawled out of prison without a dime or a hope in the world. You couldn't have gotten paroled without my assistance. I not only pleaded for you, but I took you in and taught you that there are easier ways of making a living than by stealing."

167

"The Brotherhood was my idea."

"But I've been the front. I had the background. Without my knowledge of organization, without me to stand up and hypnotize the crowd, you'd have flown off in all directions. But I not only put up with you, I worked with you and built a real organization—and now you don't like my management! I suppose they bought you Cadillacs in the penitentiary. I suppose—"

"I admit we've done pretty well," Williams stated. "I don't intend to cheat you, Pat. I'll pay you off. But the racket's mine—and I'm going to run it. I've made up my mind. Don't forget, you were just a would-be evangelist with a phoney degree until I smartened you up, and you had about as much money-sense as a cat. When I started showing you where the dough was, you were chasing around screaming about devils to a bunch of broken-down old ladies, and you weren't doing anybody any good, especially yourself. Why, the only reason you married Roy Greene was because you were half-starved and needed a meal ticket!"

"I married Roy because I wanted a man's understanding and companionship." A mocking note entered her voice. "Don't tell me you've been jealous all these years!"

"I'd just as soon sleep with a vacuum cleaner—and you know it."

"Then why wreck things?"

"I'm not wrecking a thing. It's probably hard for you to realize, but I don't need you."

"You do need me." Her inflection had a nice cutting edge. "Without protection, you'd be chased out of the city within a week."

"Stone's no protection any more. He's on his way out."

"Who told you that?" Her voice lost some of its confidence.

"Does it matter? The point, Pat, is this: The only item of any value in our relationship is the Brotherhood. It's a good cover for the girls and, solely because of that, I'm willing to make a cash settlement. I'm giving you five grand, enough so that you—"

"Five grand!" Her voice climbed shrilly. "Do you think I'm a fool? We've grossed that much in one night!"

"You're a fool if you don't take it and keep your mouth shut. Have another look at that picture. As far as getting those old bags to come in to listen to your pretty sermons is concerned, you're washed up. The picture will prove that you're a fallen woman. Whether you like it or not, you've been unfrocked, and you've lost your value to the Brotherhood. Your best bet is to take the dough and move on to other pastures."

"And let an ex-con take over?" She laughed sarcastically. "You've got another think coming, Dick. I have contacts, too, don't forget. You killed Roy. All I have to do is drop a word or two in the right places and you'll never spend another night in peace. You'll burn, Dick, as you should have years ago."

"But you'll burn, too, Pat." Dick's tone was silky. "You killed Betty Brandt, don't forget."

"How silly can you get? The girl meant nothing to me."

"Don't lie about it, Pat. We know each other well enough to lay all the cards on the table. I've known for weeks about your having the apartment at the Hidalgo Terrace. You were checking on Betty and Lucy, trying to get them to promote a second string of girls for you—in other words, you were getting ready to double-cross me. You even tried to play on Lucy's weakness by offering her a fortune in dope to set you up with a flesh ring she used to work with in Miami. But even tarts have boy friends, Pat. That's something you forgot. Lucy talked about it, and the word

169

got back to me. That's why you killed Betty. . . . She turned you down and you were afraid she'd warn me. The joke is that you killed for nothing. I already knew!"

While he talked, she sidled around until her back was toward me. She was between the light and the curtain, and her shadow deepened in front of me as though it were trying to climb into the alcove with me. I could have reached out and touched her.

"All right, Dick." A note of finality flattened her voice. "If you want this to be the end, I'll play it your way." The shadow undulated suddenly and its right arm jerked sharply. "Push the picture toward me, Dick, and no tricks. I'll shoot you through your rotten heart if you try anything."

"You're forgetting the negative, Pat. It's in a safe place."

"I'll get the negative," she retorted. "You've probably got it hidden in the same place where you've been hiding all the money you've stolen from me." What she probably intended as a chuckle came out as a treble shriek. "But I've already collected part of it, Dick—ten grand's worth. How do you like that?"

"So you tipped that jug troupe! They were no fob workers, believe me. Why, they were so smooth that I never caught on till it was all over."

"I tipped them, all right. Samp was supposed to give me a cut—but I pushed him over, and took it all."

"Sweet girl."

"Never mind. The picture, Dick. Hand it to me, slowly and easily."

"It'll do you no good." There was desperation in his voice.

"Neither will you, Dick. That's clear to me now. That's why I'm going to kill you."

I parted the curtain with my fingertips. She was standing no more than two feet from the alcove with a small automatic in her right hand. I gripped the shoe and brought it to shoulder height. Dick, looking as though he were already hearing the ringing of far-away celestial bells, was handing the photograph to her. As she snatched it from his hand, I saw her right arm tighten against her side and begin to rise.

Without conscious thought, I stepped through the curtain and hammered her behind the ear with the heel of the shoe. As she crumpled silently to the floor, a voice from the doorway said: "Nice work, Good. You saved me the trouble of drilling her."

I turned, still clutching Tina's shoe, and looked into the snub-nosed barrel of Lieutenant Mallory's pearl-handled revolver.

Fifteen

Blood From A Stone

"DOCTOR" DICK WILLIAMS released a gusty sigh. "You didn't have to wait until the last goddam moment!" he sputtered, glaring at Mallory. "She might have killed me!" He sagged in his chair like a man who has run hard and far.

Mallory kept his eyes on me. "Drop the shoe, Good. No tricks."

I eyed the gun. He held it loosely but familiarly, and it was pointed at my belly; it wouldn't require much aiming to air-condition my guts. I dropped the shoe.

A corner of his mouth twitched. "Back a step, then move to your right. There's a chair there. Sit down slowly and carefully."

I shrugged and did as directed. It was a narrow chair with stiff, wooden arms which made me feel captured. As soon as I was seated, Mallory snaked an arm down and picked up the small automatic which had fallen from Pat Greene's nerveless fingers. Without looking at it, he checked the position of the safety lock and slid the gun into the pocket of his jacket.

"I've been here for a while," Mallory said, finally addressing Dick. "I could have picked her off any time."

"She could have picked *me* off any time, too!" Williams ran a finger around the inside of his collar. "Christ, I hope this is the end of it."

"The beginning, you mean," Mallory corrected. "How much blabbing did you do in front of him?" He indicated me with a nod the size of my hopes.

"Too much, I guess." The guy eyed me as though I were a grub which had wriggled out from under a log. "I didn't know the bastard was hiding in here."

"Probably he heard the whole set-up." The cop smiled grimly. "Too bad, Good. You should have let me side-track you, as I planned; at least, you'd have had a fighting chance."

"Sure," I said. "Some chance. You intended to burn me."

"Morrie Tannen is a smart shyster. He might have got you off."

"Do you think he'll be able to get *you* off?" I asked pointedly.

"I don't intend to stick my neck out that far."

"It's already out. Besides being a crooked cop, you're the accomplice of a killer."

"We're wasting time." Mallory prodded Pat Greene's sprawled body with the toe of his shoe. "See if she's breathing, doc. If she is, tie her up and gag her."

Williams got out of his chair with alacrity, rolled her onto her back, then, with a grin, grabbed the front of her dress and ripped it down to her waist. He thrust a hand between her breasts and held it there.

Mallory snapped, "Just see if she's breathing."

"This is scientific," Dick Williams retorted. The pock marks on his thin face glistened in the reflected light. He moved his hand in an exploratory manner, then nodded judiciously. "She's breathing, all right."

"Gag her and tie her, then."

173

Williams arose, got a ball of twine from the desk, and bound her wrists. He tightened the twine cruelly, making me wince inwardly. Then, pushing her skirt unnecessarily high, he straightened her legs together and fondled her ankles.

"For chrissake," Mallory said disgustedly, "tie her and have done with it."

"Sure, sure." Williams wound the twine about her ankles, twisting it so that it cut into the pale flesh. "How's that?"

"Fine. Gag her."

"With what?"

"Your handkerchief will do." Mallory sounded impatient.

"Not mine." Dick glared up at Mallory from prune-like eyesockets. "Laundry marks, you know."

Mallory's jaw went rigid. "Then stuff a piece of her goddam dress in her mouth, you fool, before she starts screaming! Haven't we got enough trouble?"

"Good idea." Dick ripped away a portion of a lacy underslip, pried her jaws apart, forced the material between her lips. Working like a craftsman who takes pride in his skill, he grasped her thighs, pulled more of the underslip free, and tore off a long strip which he bound into place over the gag. "What about him?" he asked, leering at me.

"I'll take care of him personally," Mallory snapped. "Did Lucy get away?"

"I called her apartment. She didn't answer."

"She's probably on her way, then." Mallory deliberated a moment. "Better call the airport and check. They'll know if her seat was filled when her flight left."

"What difference does it make?" Williams asked. "She'll—"

"I want to know what's going on," Mallory said coldly. "Details may be important. Call the airport and make damned certain that she's on her way."

"Okay, okay." With jerky movements, Williams dialed the airport. A querulous note suddenly disturbed the complacency in his voice. "What's that?" he demanded. "The name is Lucy Lamaachia. She had tickets for the Miami flight . . . You're positive? . . . Could she have transferred to another flight? . . . I see . . . I see . . ." He hung up abruptly and swung violently around. "She cancelled," he announced in an elevated octave. "The clerk says a man met her and she cancelled!"

"A man met her?" Mallory repeated. He seemed to be receding to an icy planet. "What man?"

"How should I know."

In the stunned silence which followed, hope returned to me. But where was Tina, I wondered.

"Who knew she was going?" Mallory asked at last.

"No one." Dick Williams licked his lips. "Constantine did, perhaps."

"He hasn't been talking. Who else?"

"Betty."

"Somebody who isn't dead!"

"Him." Dick pointed at me.

Mallory's eyes bore into me. "Who'd you tip?" he demanded.

I grinned. "Captain Stone."

His eyes glistened meanly like a weasel's in a chicken house. "That's a lie. Stone wouldn't give credence to a shamus like you."

"Why not?" I asked. "The deal means as much to him as to you. Besides, she—" I dipped my head toward the prone figure on the floor. "—was suspicious of the doc and has been checking on him. Since Stone was a sort of partner in the racket, he knew of her suspicions and, when I confirmed them, he listened."

"No." Mallory shook his head slowly. "Stone is smarter than that. If you'd been stupid enough to go to him, he'd have knocked you off fast. You know too much. He wouldn't have dared let you loose again."

"It's possible to telephone," I said. "Stone knows my voice."

"For God's sake, Mallory, what difference does it make?" Dick cried. "They've got Lucy. All they have to do is keep her off the junk a few hours and she'll be singing! How the hell can we handle it?"

"Shut up," Mallory snapped. "Let me think a minute."

"But—"

"Shut up!"

The fake doctor subsided and, for the space of sixty agonizing seconds, Mallory stood stolidly, his gun poised and his eyes narrowed calculatingly, while I listened to my blood churn bleakly through my veins. He took a deep breath finally, like a man who has been forced to an unwilling decision, and released it slowly.

"If Good is telling the truth," he said slowly, "and if Stone has Lucy, then this whole deal will blow up fast. Tarts and junkies can't be trusted. Once they're grabbed, they'll blow their tonsils trying to get off with a suspended charge. Stone will try to take over the girls and set them up elsewhere. He'll throw all the dirt my way and get me kicked off the force." Mallory smiled tightly. "Not that that would be so bad. I've got enough salted away so that I can afford a vacation. But I'm not going to be crucified. I'm not going to let him tie me in with the killings that you insisted on, Williams."

"Me?" Dick Williams looked aghast. "It was your idea to kill Roy."

"Don't con me." Mallory's glance was frozen. "You've been carrying a torch for the Greene babe, and you wanted

176

her husband out of the way. I told you it would be simpler and safer if we knocked her off immediately, but you insisted on this picture monkey-business. I warned you it might not work. But you thought you'd have a chance to grab her for yourself, so you wouldn't play it smart. You know damned well that you've been itching to get back at her for the way she cold-shouldered you."

"Are you trying to tag me—" Dick's eyes glinted dangerously.

"You tagged yourself. Betty was your idea, too. I told you to pay her off and run her out of the city, or let somebody else handle it—but you had to play it cute. You kept her around until it was too late and this Greene dame got a line on her. Sometimes killing is necessary, but both of these could have been avoided."

"I don't like your tone, Mallory—"

"The hell with what you like, Williams." Mallory's voice snapped like a whip. "I'm drawing you a picture. If this were strictly a flesh deal, we could close shop and keep things under wraps for a while. We might even meet Stone halfway and make a deal with him. But there have been three killings! When things blow, they'll blow big and loud. The flesh racket tie-in will get a play from coast to coast. Alderman Merriam will have something new to crusade about on TV, and he'll be raking through the muck for weeks, telling the good citizens how politics and vice have corrupted the city. And the phony Brotherhood set-up is a natural for the newspapers. They'll splash pictures and sob stories about your poor betrayed believers all over the newsstands. Don't forget, Williams, you've got a record. Not even a straight pipe to the Governor will get you a pass—and you know what happens to killers in this state."

"You'll burn with me, Mallory!" Williams half rose from his chair.

177

"Sit down."

"By God, you're not ducking out and—"

With an easy fluid motion, like that of a man searching for a dollar bill in his pockets, Mallory transferred the gun to his left hand and dipped into his jacket for Pat Greene's automatic. The small gun glinted, then made a small, dry, snapping sound, like that of a piece of plate glass breaking. Dick Williams fell back into his chair, clutching his shoulder.

"Double-crossing bastard—!" Dick gasped thickly.

"I happen to need a fall guy," Mallory said stolidly. "Looks like you're elected." The automatic snapped again, then again. With a deep sigh, Dick's head dropped forward as though he were trying to look at the red stains on his chest.

I was staring at this kill-mad Mallory with horror. After a moment I managed to get hold of myself and, gulping, forced myself to speak.

"I don't get it," I said.

"Why not?" Mallory asked. "One thing about being a cop, you learn how to keep a clean trail. An ex-con like Williams would rat if he got the chance. I can think on my feet. That's why I'm a lieutenant of detectives."

"I still don't get it," I said. "You've got Captain Stone, Doctor Greene, Lucy Lamaachia, and me left—and you can't kill all of us. You're heading straight for the chair."

"Lucy is out of this. Even if she talks, no jury will believe a junkie. Stone can be dealt with. When he sees how things lie, he'll keep his eyes on the fast buck and make a deal with me." Mallory sounded as though things were already cut and dried. "You and Greene are my only remaining problems and, considering that picture which Williams arranged to have taken, it doesn't look to me like it's going to be tough."

178

"Was it he who knocked me on the head after I found Betty dead?"

"His boys did it. They doped the Greene dame and put her in bed with you—then took pictures, with Roy Greene dead practically under the bed."

"But that tin of horse—"

"I told you once, remember? Roy was planning to turn over that dope in exchange for some flesh . . . Don't try it, Good!"

He must have read my intentions in my eyes. I slackened my muscles, admitting to myself hopelessly that Mallory was too wary to be jumped.

"All right," he said, waving his own gun, the gun in his left hand. "Untie her, Good. I don't want her marked up too much."

"Why?"

"Hurry. Do as I say." Both guns looked at my belly.

I got down on my knees and fumbled with the knotted twine. Williams had done a good job. I broke two fingernails getting the knots open. When I pulled the gag from her mouth, she moaned and licked her lips weakly.

"Get back, now," Mallory directed. As I backed toward the chair, he stepped toward her, and, holding the muzzle of the automatic directly over her heart, he pumped two bullets into her. She shivered once, as though Death's breath was chilly, then lay still.

"You're insane!" I gasped hoarsely.

"Smart, not insane," Mallory's eyes were opaque and glinted like metal. With a contemptuous gesture, he rubbed the automatic against his jacket then tossed it onto the floor beside Pat Greene's body. "That picture is a good gimmick: You were mixed up with the Greene woman, trying to get your fingers into the racket she was working, and Doctor Dick found out about it. Like the good, righteous, man he

179

was, he cornered the two of you here and threatened Greene with exposure. During the argument, you pulled a gun and shot him. She tried to stop you—and you shot her, too. It's the old triangle set-up, but this time with a picture and a Gospel choir. It'll go over big."

"You'll have a sweet time explaining the gun," I said. "No private dick carries that kind of a rod."

"So maybe she pulled it out and you tried to get it away from her." Mallory shrugged. "It'll hold together. People won't worry much about anything except the fact that it's a juicy triangle situation with plenty of blood."

"You intend to kill me too, then."

"Of course." He smiled. "With you out of the way, everything will be wrapped up neat. Thanks to you, I even know where the tin of dope is. I'll pick it up at my convenience and peddle it for a small fortune. And killing you is no risk at all. It's strictly in the line of duty. Maybe I'll even get a citation or a captaincy for doing it."

"Maybe that cop of yours, Russin, will talk."

"Never mind him. He's on my side." His big gun was in his right hand now. He firmed the barrel in line with my stomach. "That's enough conversation. So long, Good—"

Somewhere nearby a woman screamed.

Mallory's mouth opened.

From outside the building there came a faint crash, then a tumbling rattle of hollow metal. Mallory stiffened.

"What's that?" he cracked.

A large caliber pistol fired twice.

I thought: *Tina. Oh, God . . .*

Then, in the split second that his head turned to listen, I leaped at him.

Sixteen

The Last Stall

HIS GUN ROARED. Flame seared my side, then my hands were on his arm, sliding toward his wrist in an attempt to twist it viciously. It was a commando trick, one designed to disarm the enemy quickly and efficiently. But he was smart. Instead of jerking back, as an armed man normally would, he leaned toward me, following the direction of the twist and minimizing its efficacy. At the same instant, he chopped the edge of his left hand toward my neck. I saw the blow coming, rolled my shoulder into its path, and, as it pounded a spike of pain into my back, I gripped his arm and wrenched at it with all my strength.

He cursed and went sprawling on the floor, still clutching the gun. I landed on him before he could fire at me, and we rolled over and over, each searching for an instant of vulnerability or weakness. The gun was paramount in his mind and, as we twisted and strained, he clung to it stubbornly and concentrated on getting its muzzle pointed toward my body. I was acutely conscious of its deadly proximity. With a strength born of desperation, I tortured his arm trying to force him to release the weapon.

My hands slipped once and the gun plunged up and down

in a vicious blow at my head. I kneed him and stabbed spread fingers at his eyes, feeling him writhe with pain at the same instant that the gun descended. The blow seemed to shatter my head. During the brief dazzle of color which followed, I tasted the salt of blood on my lips. I kneed him again and caught his wrist. Muscles rippled under my fingers as, tensing his shoulders mightily, he tried to raise the gun and aim it into my ear. Sweat poured down my back and the room seemed to revolve dizzily about me.

Another gun fired outside the building and someone shouted.

Far away a siren's wail rose eerily.

Mallory shifted suddenly and his gun moved closer to my head. I shook sweat from my eyes and saw the triumphant smirk that glistened on his taut lips. I flung my weight against his arm, trying to deflect it for an instant, but it was like trying to move a beam imbedded in concrete. The gun moved imperceptibly but certainly toward my ear as my grasp began to weaken.

The stairway rattled with heavy feet.

I kicked desperately and felt my shoe collide with flesh and bone. I remembered Pat Greene's body—and the automatic which Mallory had flung beside her. Clinging to his arm with renewed hope, I tried to recall how many shots had been fired. Three bullets for Dr. Dick. Two for the Greene dame. That left one load, possibly two, in the small gun. I heaved upward, praying for a second's grace before Mallory's weapon exploded and blew me into infinity; then I released his arm, rolled across his chest and face, and clawed for the automatic.

He twisted like an infuriated cat and came up on his knees, clutching the gun and grinning like a maniac. He raised the muzzle.

But a shout filled the room. And I saw Captain Stone,

holding a Police Positive in his fist, filling the doorway.

Mallory saw him at the same instant I did and with a scream like a betrayed virgin he swung his gun in Stone's direction. Stone, with a smile full of flowers, the kind they strew over coffins, jerked his fist and the Police Positive roared twice. Mallory stiffened, dropped his gun, and rose a few inches. Then he collapsed. Still smiling, Stone looked at me. I saw the purpose in his eyes and felt the automatic in my hand recoil as I squeezed the trigger.

A surprised look smoothed some of the flushed excitement from Stone's face. Like a man sleep-walking, he took a step toward me. I squeezed the trigger again, waiting for the expected cracking sound of its discharge, but it was flooded away in a wave of running feet and hoarse shouts. Stone took another step toward me, bending his knees slightly, and his blue uniform seemed to balloon up and around me, knocking me back and down and enveloping me . . . and then I blacked out.

An arm cradled my neck, torturing my shoulder, and a familiar voice kept repeating: "Carl? Carl? . . ."

From far away a voice groaned: "Yeah . . ."

"It's Morrie, Carl. Everything's fine. The doc says you're all right."

"Yeah," I groaned. "Fine."

"We got there in time, thank God! Think you can sit up?"

"Sure." I gasped my lungs full of air. "Where am I?"

"Augustana Hospital."

"Oh." The whiteness which had been spinning in front of my eyes steadied and I recognized an iron cot, sheets, white walls. "Tina?" I asked weakly.

"Stone and Mallory are dead," Morrie said. I moved my head so I could stare into the thick lenses of his glasses. "The Greene woman and Williams are dead, too. But I suppose you know that. If it hadn't been for Captain Stone, we might not have found you. He led the Commissioner's men to that hall."

"Tina?" I repeated.

"When you didn't call back, I got worried," Morrie went on. His round face glistened with sweat, I noticed. "I told the Commissioner that you'd mentioned the Brotherhood. He dispatched a squad to the Chicago Avenue Station, and, just as they pulled up, a car with Captain Stone in it went highballing north. The Commissioner ordered it followed, and that's how——"

"Morrie!" I interrupted harshly. "Tina. *Where's Tina!*"

Morrie moistened his lips and swallowed. "She's down at the Brotherhood hall, Carl," he said quietly.

"Shot?"

He nodded.

"Who did it?"

"Stone. She managed to tell me, before she passed out——"

"What else did she say?"

"When he broke in, she was letting out a scream—to divert Mallory's attention from you. Stone shot her down—probably figured that if she was in the hall with you two, she must have known too much. Or maybe it was just sheer reflex on his part."

"Help me up!"

"You've got to stay in bed a while, Carl. You're banged up a little."

"Help me up!"

"Please, Carl. Lie down. The hospital——"

The room swam around me and I heard someone cursing wildly. It sounded like my voice. But it couldn't be my voice because Mallory had the gun and was trying to point it into my ear and Pat Greene sprawled on the floor dead with blood all over her and I couldn't move his arm. . . .

184

A kindly-faced man with twinkly glasses balanced on his narrow nose was peering down at me while his fingers held my wrist firmly. Behind him there was a larger man, a man in a shiny blue serge suit who had an anxious look on his big face. Reason tugged at me. The one with glasses was a doctor. The big one was Timothy Spellman, the Commissioner of Police. The pictures I'd seen of him were lousy. They'd made him look like a politician; now, standing with his hands resting on the foot of the iron cot, he looked tired and ordinary and human.

"You'd better restrain him," Morrie's voice said from the other side of the bed. "I know him. He won't stay put until he's seen her."

"Seen who?" the doctor asked. He removed his fingers from my wrist.

"The girl."

"Oh." The doctor pursed his lips, then nodded. "Well, there's nothing seriously wrong with him. His heart is strong. He needs rest badly, though. It might be wise to let him see her."

"But, doctor—!" Morrie protested.

"She's in the hospital, now, and . . ."

"I know—but the strain—"

"He needn't walk," the doctor said with professional finality. "I'll have a wheelchair sent in. One of you can take him in for a minute. By then, the shot I gave him will begin to take effect and he'll be able to relax and rest." He turned toward the door. "I'll speak to the nurse."

I closed my eyes and waited.

Morrie and a nurse helped me into a wheelchair. Commissioner Spellman turned the chair carefully and pushed me into the hall. The air in the hall smelled strongly of iodoform and ether. I sucked it into my lungs, hoping it

185

would disinfect some of the thoughts which swirled through my mind. Then the chair was going through a narrow doorway into a dimly lighted white room. My heart throbbed in my throat and tears blurred my eyes as I saw the cot where she lay.

Spellman turned the chair and brought me alongside her. Her eyes were closed and someone had brushed her thick blonde hair away from her face so that it lay like an amber cloud on the white pillow.

"Go away," I muttered fiercely. I clenched my hands and pounded them on the arms of the chair. "Go away!"

"All right, Carl." Spellman sounded as though he understood. He went out of the room, closing the door.

"Tina," I murmured. "I'm here, Tina."

Her lips seemed to smile.

I felt for her hand and touched her cool fingertips. "I guess everything is going to be all right, Tina," I said softly. "Morrie talked to the Commissioner, and the Commissioner's squad tailed Stone to the Brotherhood. But there was a lot of shooting, a hell of a lot of shooting, and a lot of crooked cops are crawling for cover. But the worst ones are dead: Stone and Mallory. And the phony doctors are dead, too—along with their horrible 'charity' racket."

She seemed to nod.

"I guess you were meant to be a stall, Tina," I whispered. "It doesn't make much difference what a person does with his life as long as he does it with all his heart. It isn't hard to love a person like that, darling. Maybe you didn't know what you were doing, but you stalled them, Tina. You stalled Mallory even slicker than you did the the man in black in front of the bank, while Samp was walking away with the loot. This time my life was the loot—and you let me walk away with it." My throat choked. "I don't know how to say it, Tina, but I'm grateful . . . and proud."

HYMN TO HELL

Her features softened and her fingers seemed to tighten on mine.

"I guess that's all, kid."

I sat there, holding her hand and sensing the aura of peace and contentment which surrounded her; then, feeling suddenly older and wearier, I fumbled for the wheels and reluctantly turned the chair away from her.

At the door, I turned and looked back.

She didn't wave, she didn't move.

I rolled away slowly . . . and forever.

— THE END —

GLOSSARY OF TERMS DRAWN FROM THIEVES' ARGOT, AS USED IN THIS BOOK

BING—A verb, usually; *to bing,* meaning to rob.

CANNON—A professional pickpocket.

DIP—The act of searching a victim's pocket.

DOUBLE SUCKER—A victim who, after being robbed, doesn't call the cops.

FINGER—Point out or indicate the victim to be robbed.

FOB WORKER—A novice pickpocket who is capable only of robbing small-change pockets.

FUZZ—The police.

GRIFT SENSE—The ability to think ahead of a sucker, to sense what he will do next.

HANGER—A lady's pocketbook.

HEELED—Has money.

HORSE—Heroin.

JUG—Bank.

JUG TROUPE—A group of thieves which specializes in the robbing of bank patrons.

KICK—Pockets.

MARK—Victim.

MOLL BUZZERS—Pickpockets who specialize in robbing women.

PATCH—The outside pocket of a jacket or coat.

PIT WORKER—The highest type of pickpocket, one who specializes in stealing from inner pockets of coats, vests etc.

ROUSTER TYPE—One who befriends drunks for the purpose of robbing them.

RUMBLES—Touches a victim with deliberate awkwardness to learn how alert the victim is and how he may react.

SNEAK TYPE—One who robs furtively, usually in subways or on park benches.

STALLS—Members of a troupe whose job is to distract the sucker while "the wire" operates.

SPOT—Locate or designate.

STIFF—A folded newspaper, used either to conceal the hands of the thief while he's working or to conceal the loot as it is removed.

SUCKER—A person like you or me.

TIP-OFF—A signal, manual or oral, used to spot a well-heeled sucker.

WIRE—The member of a troupe who does the actual stealing.